# The Táin

# THE
# TÁIN

## A NEW
## TRANSLATION OF THE
## TÁIN BÓ CÚAILNGE

## CIARAN
## CARSON

VIKING

VIKING
Published by the Penguin Group
Penguin Group (USA) Inc., 375 Hudson Street,
New York, New York 10014, U.S.A.
Penguin Group (Canada), 90 Eglinton Avenue East, Suite 700,
Toronto, Ontario, Canada M4P 2Y3
(a division of Pearson Penguin Canada Inc.)
Penguin Books Ltd, 80 Strand, London WC2R 0RL, England
Penguin Ireland, 25 St. Stephen's Green, Dublin 2, Ireland
(a division of Penguin Books Ltd)
Penguin Books Australia Ltd, 250 Camberwell Road, Camberwell,
Victoria 3124, Australia
(a division of Pearson Australia Group Pty Ltd)
Penguin Books India Pvt Ltd, 11 Community Centre, Panchsheel Park,
New Delhi – 110 017, India
Penguin Group (NZ), 67 Apollo Drive, Rosedale, North Shore 0632,
New Zealand (a division of Pearson New Zealand Ltd)
Penguin Books (South Africa) (Pty) Ltd, 24 Sturdee Avenue,
Rosebank, Johannesburg 2196, South Africa

Penguin Books Ltd, Registered Offices:
80 Strand, London WC2R 0RL, England

First American edition
Published in 2008 by Viking Penguin,
a member of Penguin Group (USA) Inc.

1 2 3 4 5 6 7 8 9 10

Translation and editorial material copyright © Ciaran Carson, 2007
All rights reserved

LIBRARY OF CONGRESS CATALOGING IN PUBLICATION DATA

Táin bó Cúailnge. English.
The Táin / translated and with an introduction by Ciaran Carson.
p. cm.
ISBN 978-0-670-01868-0
1. Epic literature, Irish—Translations into English. 2. Tales—Ireland—Translations into
English. 3. Cuchulain (Legendary character)—Legends. 4. Medb (Legendary character)—
Legends. 5. Mythology, Celtic—Ireland. I. Carson, Ciaran, 1948– II. Title.
PB1423.T3C37 2008
398.2209415—dc22
2007037999

Printed in the United States of America

In memory of the storyteller John Campbell
of Mullaghbawn, Co. Armagh,
born 1933, died 2006

# Contents

# Acknowledgements

I am first of all most grateful to Marcella Edwards of Penguin Classics, whose idea it was to commission this translation. It would never have occurred to me otherwise. Thanks are due to Liam Breatnach, Greg Toner and Michael Cronin, who provided me with useful reading lists of background and critical material. Conversations with Bob Welch, Aodán Mac Póilin and Brian Mullen helped me to clarify some aspects of the translation. My wife Deirdre read the work in progress, as she has done with all my work since we met some thirty years ago; as always, her response and her suggestions were invaluable.

# Introduction

*Táin Bó Cúailnge* is the longest and most important tale in
the Ulster Cycle, a group of some eighty interrelated stories
which recount the exploits of the Ulaid, a prehistoric people
of the north of Ireland, from whom the name of Ulster derives.
The authors of these stories are anonymous. Briefly, the *Táin*
tells of how Queen Medb of Connacht, envious that her
husband Ailill owns a prize bull, Finnbennach the White-
horned, the superior of any that she possesses, decides to go
on an expedition to steal the *Donn Cúailnge*, the Brown Bull
of Cooley, in the province of Ulster. At this time the Ulstermen
are laid low by an ancient, periodic curse[1] which renders them
unfit for battle, and the defence of the province is undertaken
by Cú Chulainn. At the beginning of the *Táin* Cú Chulainn
is a shadowy figure, but he gradually emerges as its chief
protagonist, a figure of immense physical, supernatural and
verbal resource who engaged the attention of many later
Irish and Anglo-Irish writers. By a series of guerrilla tactics,
chariot-fighting and single combat, he holds off the Connacht
army until the Ulstermen recover. Fer Diad, Cú Chulainn's
best friend, is tricked by Medb into challenging him to single
combat and is killed by Cú Chulainn. A final battle ensues.
Medb and her forces are defeated. The two bulls clash. They
die fighting each other, and a peace is made between Ulster
and Connacht. Such are the bare bones of the story; its origins,
its transmission and the modus operandi of its authors are a

more complicated matter, and have been the subject of much scholarly debate.

There are several legends, or versions of the same legend, concerning the transmission of the *Táin*. A typical example is that given by Maghnus Ó Domhnaill, a lord of Donegal, in his account of the life of St Colm Cille, written under Ó Domhnaill's direction at his castle in Lifford in 1532. The story, referring to events of some 900 years earlier, can be summarized as follows:

Senchan the High Bard of Erin comes to stay with Gúaire, a prince of Connacht, together with his entourage of three fifties of master poets and three fifties of apprentices, each and every one of them with two women and a servant and a dog. They eat him out of house and home, since Gúaire is forced to gratify their every whim for fear of satire. When Gúaire's brother, the hermit Marbán, hears of this he curses them, taking away their gift of poetry until such times as they can recite the whole of the *Táin*. For a year and a day they scour Ireland interviewing bards and storytellers in search of the *Táin*, with no success, for only fragments of that long story survive. At last Senchan goes to Colm Cille, who takes him to the grave of Fergus Mac Róich, one of the chief protagonists of the *Táin*. Fergus, summoned from the grave by Colm Cille, proceeds to narrate the whole story, which is written down by St Ciaran of Cluain on the hide of his pet dun cow: hence *Lebor na hUidre*, 'The Book of the Dun Cow'.

This story is an allusion to another famous legend concerning Colm Cille himself: admiring a certain book belonging to St Finnen, Colm Cille asks him if he can copy it; the book deserves a wider audience. Finnen refuses. Colm Cille secretly copies the book anyway. According to Ó Domhnaill, the room in which Colm Cille works is illuminated by the five fingers of his hand, which blaze like five candles. Colm Cille is spied on by a youth, who, attracted by the preternatural light, peers through a hole in the church door, whereupon his eye is plucked out by Colm Cille's pet crane. The youth goes to Finnen, who restores the eye. (I note in passing that a plausible etymology for Finnen is 'fair bird'.) Finnen disputes Colm Cille's right to the copy, and the two clerics ask Diarmaid, the High King, to resolve the issue, whereupon he makes what has been called the first copyright judgment: 'To every cow her calf; to every book its copy.' For books then were, quite literally, made from calves, as borne out by the English word 'vellum', from Old French *vel*, a calf.

As it happens, the book known to us as *Lebor na hUidre* or 'The Book of the Dun Cow' – now in the keeping of the Royal Irish Academy in Dublin – does indeed contain a partial version of the *Táin*, as well as an account of the life of Colm Cille; but this text (of which only 67 vellum leaves survive from a total of some 130) was written in the year 1100 or so, and not in the sixth century when Colm Cille lived. However, it is thought that much of 'The Book of the Dun Cow' is derived from texts of the ninth century, now no longer extant, which might in turn have been based on texts of two or three centuries earlier. But we cannot know to what extent these putative antecedents were based on oral accounts which would themselves have been transmitted in several versions, changed, improved or corrupted as they were recounted by different storytellers with different historical, cultural and artistic agendas.

So it is with the *Táin* itself, which has been collated as two main versions or recensions. Recension I is a marriage of the *Lebor na hUidre* text and another partial but complementary text found in the fourteenth-century 'Yellow Book of Lecan'. It is made up of several linguistic strata, and includes many interpolations, re-writings, palimpsests, redundancies, rep-etitions, narrative contradictions and lacunae: evidence, per-haps, that this version of the *Táin* was compiled from an oral tradition which would include variant performances. Recen-sion II, found in the twelfth-century 'Book of Leinster', is an attempt to present a more unified narrative. It contains the introductory 'Pillow Talk' episode absent from Recension I, as well as a much fuller account of Cú Chulainn's combat with Fer Diad. Although it resolves many of the inconsistencies, and has been deemed a more 'literary' version by many commentators, Recension II often has a florid and prolix style less congenial to modern taste than the laconic force of Recension I.

Frank O'Connor[2] has called the *Táin* 'a simply appalling text . . . endlessly scribbled over', and its interpretation 'a task better suited to the archaeologist than the literary critic, because it is like an excavation that reveals a dozen habitation sites'. The *Táin* might well be an archaeological site, but it need not be an appalling prospect. One could equally well see it as a magnificently ruined cathedral, whose fabric displays the ravages of war, fashion and liturgical expediency: a compendium of architectural interpolations, erasures, deliberate archaisms, renovations and restorations; a space inhabited by many generations, each commenting on their predecessors. Or one can see the *Táin* as an exemplar of what has been called 'the supple stylistic continuum'[3] of early Irish writing, a fluid mix of poetry and prose. The prose itself can be separated into three main stylistic strands: the straightforward, laconic style of the general narrative and dialogue, particularly evident in the earliest version of the *Táin*; a formulaic style found primarily in descriptive passages, especially where an observer describes a distant scene to an audience; and an alliterative, heavily adjectival style typical of the later writing. The poetry, which is rhymed and syllabic in form, is spoken by characters at certain heightened points of the action. The *Táin* also includes passages of the genre known as *rosc* (pl. *roscada*), or 'rhetorics'. These are by far the most problematic elements in the text, and may represent its earliest linguistic stratum. They might, however, include deliberate archaisms. They are usually marked in the manuscripts by '.r.' in the margin, indicating that the medieval scribes recognized them as a distinct formal element. They are written as continuous blocks of unpunctuated rhythmic prose, densely alliterative and syntactically ambiguous. It has been suggested that they might in fact be poems written to archaic metrical principles, using a stressed rather than a syllabic line. Whatever the case, their gnomic quality has resisted translation until comparatively recently. Whether their obscurity is due to unintentional or deliberate garbling is open to debate. *Roscada*, like the verse in the *Táin*, are spoken by characters in the course of the action, and can at times be interpreted as verbal jousting or an exchange of veiled threats: a good example is the dialogue between Ailill and Fergus just after Cuilluis, Ailill's charioteer, has stolen Fergus's sword.

The *Táin*, then, is a compilation of various styles.[4] In this context one might dwell on the range of possible meanings embodied in the Irish word *táin*. The Irish title *Táin Bó Cúailnge* has been translated as 'The Cattle Raid of Cooley', and *táin* can indeed mean an act of capturing or driving off, a raid, a foray, or the story of such an exploit. There are seven such tales in the Ulster cycle, known collectively as *tána*: they thus constitute a genre. But *táin* can also mean a large gathering of people, an assembly, a conglomeration, a procedure. Without stretching it too much, one could say that *táin* can mean a compilation or anthology of stories and verse, which is precisely what the *Táin* is: words captured on calf-skin. The naming of *Táin Bó Cúailnge* thus enacts and embodies its own narrative and scribal procedures.

The *Táin* is obsessed by topography, by place-names and their etymologies. Or rather, their alleged etymologies, for many if not most of the stories behind the names are retrospective inventions: by virtue of narrative licence, they come after the names and not before them. Some of the place-names might not exist at all, but are literary fictions, created for the greater glory or shame of whatever hero fought or died in that imagined realm, or to commemorate whatever foul or noble deed occurred there. A typically laconic example goes as follows:

Lethan came to his ford on the river Níth in Conaille. Galled by Cú Chulainn's deeds, he lay in wait for him. Cú Chulainn cut off his head and left it with the body. Hence the name Áth Lethan, Lethan's Ford.

A likely story, we might say, given the fact that the most obvious meaning of *Áth Lethan* is 'broad ford'. But we are taken in by the narrative drive, for this is one of a series of such encounters, and for that moment we summon up a warrior called Lethan, 'the Broad'. And we note that the ford is 'his' even before he comes to it. His fate is predicated by the name. After his death he pays no further part in the story, but the story renders him memorable. He becomes an item in the landscape of the *Táin*, embodied in its elaborate *dindsenchas*, 'the lore of high places'.

That mode of thinking, of landscape as a mnemonic map, is still current in Ireland. I once had the privilege of accompanying the late Paddy Tunney on a car journey through his native County Fermanagh. Known as 'The Man of Songs', Tunney was a living thesaurus of stories, songs, poems and recitations, and as we drove through this townland or that, passing by otherwise unremarkable farmsteads or small hedgy fields or stretches of bog, by this lake or that river or well-head, he would relate their history, lilt an accompanying reel or jig, or sing snatches of the songs that sprang from that source, and tell stories of the remarkable characters who once dwelt there.[5] I have no idea how many thousands of words were thus encompassed in that extraordinary memory of his, but I do know that for him place, story and song were intimately and dynamically connected, and that his landscape spoke volumes. Entering it at any point led to immense narrative consequences.

Indeed, we might address some of the alleged deficiencies of the *Táin* as a text if we consider it not as a straightforward story-line running from A to B, but as a journey through a landscape, with all sorts of interesting detours to be taken off

the main route, like a series of songs with variant airs. My
foray with Paddy Tunney into Fermanagh was, like the *Táin*,
a compendium of different genres – storytelling, verse, song,
speculation about the origin of this place-name or that.
Another journey on another day would have produced different results, or similar results differently ordered. The landscape is a source-book. So it must have been for the authors
and the audience of the *Táin*. Each would have been familiar
with the general lie of the land, and some would have been
more knowledgeable than others with regard to one or
another detail of its topography. Different performers would
treat its various elements differently. There would have been
a few master navigators, like Tunney, who had the whole map
in their heads. So I have no difficulty with the proposition,
disparaged by some scholars with no experience of a living
oral culture, that a narrative of *Táin*-like dimensions could
have existed in several or many oral versions. The prodigious
memory of some preliterate or illiterate individuals is well
attested. That is not to deny the interaction of oral and literate
cultures which began with the arrival of Christianity in Ireland.
One must have influenced the other.

   In this context the story of how St Ciaran writes down the
*Táin* at the dictation of Fergus can be seen as a parable of the
superiority of Christian learning over mere Irish pagan lore:
as if to say, even your own history is unreliable, recorded in
the fickle human memory, whereas our words, inscribed in
books and their copies, shall flourish and survive unaltered
for all time. The monkish redactor of the 'Book of Leinster'
felt compelled to add to the end of the *Táin*, 'a blessing on
everyone who shall faithfully memorize the *Táin* as it is written here and shall not add any other form to it'. He both
disparages and privileges the art of memory. He writes that
sentence in Irish, the language of the lay person, and then
adds in Latin, the language of the cleric:

> But I who have written down this story (*historia*) or rather this
> fable, give no credence to the story, or fable. For some things
> in it are demonic deceptions, and others poetic figments; some
> are possible, and others not; while still others are for the enter-
> tainment of idiots (*delectationem stultorem*).

The shift in language is telling. This is a man who dwells in
both languages, and the pagan and the Christian worlds they
represent. He has a foot in both camps. He wades in a ford
of meaning.

Much of the action in the *Táin* takes place at fords. The Irish
for 'ford', *áth*, is cognate with Latin *vado*, 'I go' and English
'wade'. There are deep ends to these fords. In Irish mythology,
streams and rivers are liminal zones between this world and the
Otherworld. The cry of the Banshee is commonly heard near
flowing water, and in Gaelic-speaking Scotland the Banshee is
known as the *Bean-nighe*, the Washerwoman at the Ford, who
washes the grave-clothes of those about to die. In the *Táin*, the
ford is a metaphysical space, a portal and a barrier, a place of
challenge, a border between Cú Chulainn and the rest of
Ireland. Or, as we have seen, it represents a twilight zone –
and there are many such twilights in the *Táin* – between the
pagan and the Christian worlds. The young Cú Chulainn
overhears the druid and seer Cathbad pronouncing that if a
warrior took up arms on that day, his name would endure in
Ireland as a byword for heroic deeds, and that stories about
him would be told forever. Whereupon Cú Chulainn rushes
to the king and asks him for arms. He recognizes that deeds
can never achieve fame without their being recounted in
words. History is made up of story. The druid's corollary
when he sees him taking up arms, that the life of such a
warrior would be short, means nothing to him. His death will
be his salvation. Midway through the *Táin* Cú Chulainn falls
nearly mortally wounded and is made to rise again, like Christ
at Easter, after a sleep of three days. In some versions of an
ancillary tale, 'The Death of Cú Chulainn', he dies, like Christ,

aged thirty-three. Cú Chulainn's heroic life and death can be read as a perfect Christian life, for all the slaughter it entails.

Some scholars have suggested that early Irish prose might have been modelled on the narrative procedures of the Lives of the Saints – hagiographies such as that of Colm Cille, which contain episodes as impossible, or miraculous, as any related in the *Táin* – but it is at least as valid to argue that early hagiographies were modelled on folk tales, or that they are a type of folklore. In any event the two are inextricably connected. A case in point is the tale *Siaburcharput Con Culainn* ('The Phantom Chariot of Cú Chulainn'), in which St Patrick attempts to convert Láegaire Mac Crimthann, high king of Tara, to Christianity. The king refuses, unless Patrick can resurrect Cú Chulainn in his chariot. The saint does so; Cú Chulainn appears and describes the hell to which he, as a pagan, is confined, whereupon Mac Crimthann immediately asks to be baptized. For his co-operation Cú Chulainn, his charioteer and horses are allowed into heaven. Interestingly, Colm Cille (actually a nickname meaning 'Church Dove') was baptized Crimthann, or 'fox', and as a canine figure he can be linked to Cú Chulainn, the Hound of Culann. It is perhaps no accident that both saint and pagan hero are abbreviated as 'CC' in medieval manuscripts. Both Colm Cille and Cú Chulainn are warriors; they are both accomplished poets, and proficient in ogam script; both are associated with cranes; and both have superhuman powers.

Such interweaving of pagan myth and Christianity is exemplified by another story in the Ulster Cycle in which Conchobar, King of Ulster and foster-father of Cú Chulainn, dies at the same time as Christ. Indeed, it was once thought that the 'events' of the Ulster Cycle did indeed take place around the time of Christ, but it is now accepted that such a chronology is an invention of the clerical redactors of the stories, and it is perhaps more useful to think of these narratives as existing in an imaginative realm rather than in any definite historical period. However, there may be some justification for seeing

the *Táin* as 'a window into the Iron Age'.[6] Whether or not it
is an Irish Iron Age is another question. For instance, it is
undeniable that the social and warfaring practices embedded
in the narrative bear remarkable similarities to those of the
Gauls or 'Celts'[7] of continental Europe, as described by
Diodorus Siculus in around 60 BC:

> In their journeyings and when they go into battle the Gauls use
> chariots drawn by two horses, which carry the charioteer and
> the warrior . . . They first hurl their javelins at the enemy and
> then step down from their chariots and join battle with their
> swords. Certain of them despise death to such a degree that
> they enter the perils of battle with no more than a girdle about
> their loins . . . It is also their custom . . . to step out in front of
> the line and challenge the most valiant men from among their
> opponents to single combat, brandishing their weapons in front
> of them to terrify their adversaries. And when any man accepts
> the challenge to battle, they then beak forth into a song of
> praise of the valiant deeds of their ancestors and in boast of
> their own high achievements, reviling all the while and belitt-
> ling their opponent, and trying, in a word, by such talk to strip
> him of his bold spirit before the combat.[8]

The passage is especially telling when one considers that for
all the chariot-fighting in the *Táin*, the archaeological evidence
for chariots in Ireland is almost entirely lacking. As Barry
Cunliffe puts it, 'While it is as well to remember the old
archaeological adage that absence of evidence is not evidence
of absence, the possibility must be allowed that chariots were
never a feature of Irish Iron Age society.'[9]

Whatever the case, the chief attraction of the *Táin* lies not
in the ultimately insoluble problem of its origins, but in its
tremendous artistic power. In its abrupt shifts from laconic
brutality to moments of high poetry and deep pathos, from
fantastic and vividly imagined description to darkly obscure
utterance, from tragedy to black humour, it has no parallel in

Irish literature, with the possible exception of another multi-layered, polyphonic tale, James Joyce's *Ulysses*.

## NOTES

1. See pp. 216–17, note 3.
2. In *A Short History of Irish Literature: a Backward Look* (New York: 1967).
3. Patricia Kelly, in J. P. Mallory (ed.), *Aspects of The Táin* (Belfast: 1992).
4. For a comprehensive analysis, see Maria Tymoczo, *Translation in a Postcolonial Context* (Manchester: 1999).
5. Paddy Tunney died in 2002, aged 81. Some notion of his repertoire and procedures may be gleaned from his books, *The Stone Fiddle: My Way to Traditional Song* and *Where Songs Do Thunder: Travels in Traditional Song* (both Belfast: 1991).
6. See Kenneth Hurlstone Jackson, *The Oldest Irish Tradition: A Window on the Iron Age* (Cambridge: 1964).
7. I use the term advisedly. For an examination of the concept of 'Celticness' see Barry Cunliffe, *The Celts: A Very Short Introduction* (Oxford: 2003).
8. *Diodorus of Sicily*, with an English translation by C. H. Oldfather (London: 1934).
9. Barry Cunliffe, *The Celts*.

# Further Reading

## Translations

Thomas Kinsella's *The Táin* is widely available. Cecile O'Rahilly's editions *Táin Bó Cúailnge from the Book of Leinster*, and *Táin Bó Cúailnge Recension I* (Dublin, 1967 and 1976) carry English translations. The texts may be ordered by emailing the publishers, the Dublin Institute of Advanced Studies, at book-orders@admin.dias.ie. Lady Gregory's *Cuchulain of Muirthemne* (reprinted, Gerrards Cross, 1970) contains much of the *Táin* narrative in a mixture of translation and paraphrase. Patrick Brown's website at www.paddybrown.co.uk has good colloquial translations-cum-paraphrases of some of the Ulster Cycle stories, including the *Táin*. Also available online are Winfred Faraday's 1904 translation of Recension I at www.yorku.ca/inpar/tain_faraday.pdf and Joseph Dunn's 1914 translation of Recension II at (http://vassun.vassar.edu/~sttaylor/cooley/). 'The Book of Leinster' text was first edited and published by Ernst Windisch as *Die altirische Heldensaga Táin Bó Cúalnge nach dem Book von Leinster*, with his German translation (Leipzig, 1905). There is a French translation by Henri d'Arbois de Jubainville, *Táin Bó Cúalnge, Enlèvement du taureau divin et des vaches de Cooley* (Paris, 1907).

# Critical Studies

Two very useful compilations are J. P. Mallory (ed.), *Aspects of the Táin* (Belfast, 1992); and J. P. Mallory and Gerard Stockman (eds.), *Ulidia: Proceedings of the First International Conference on the Ulster Cycle of Tales* (Belfast, 1994). Kenneth Hurlstone Jackson's *The Oldest Irish Tradition: A Window on the Iron Age* (Cambridge, 1964) is much referred to in the literature. Maria Tymoczo's *Translation in a Postcolonial Context* (Manchester, 1999) is a brilliant study of the cultural politics of translation with special reference to the *Táin*.

# Background Reading

Barry Cunliffe's *The Celts: A Very Short Introduction* (Oxford, 2003) is the best introduction to the topic, elegantly written and containing a great deal of information in a small space. Useful reference works are James McKillop, *Dictionary of Celtic Mythology* (Oxford, 1998) and Dáithí Ó hÓgáin, *The Lore of Ireland* (Cork, 2006). Simon James, *Exploring the World of the Celts* (London, 2005) is accessible and attractively illustrated.

# A Note on the Translation

In 1969 Dolmen Press of Dublin published *The Táin*, translated from the Irish by Thomas Kinsella, with brush drawings by Louis de Brocquy, in an edition of 1,750 copies. It was immediately hailed as a classic for the vibrancy of the translation and the magnificence of its graphic accompaniment. A mass-market edition was published by Oxford University Press a year later. Its cultural impact was immense.[1] No easily accessible translation of the work had existed until then. Those that did were mostly rendered in a dutiful translatorese that did little justice to the dynamism of the original; the poetry was written as prose, and the problematic *rosc* passages were left mostly untranslated. The title alone, sometimes rendered as 'The Cattle Raid of Cooley' was decidedly offputting, suggesting a dime Western rather than an epic.[2] Kinsella's radical decision to combine the English definite article with the key Irish word offered a parallel with national epics such as the *Mahabharata*, the *Mabinogion*, the *Iliad* and the *Odyssey*, and so on. Other parallels were made: appearing as it did at an especially violent period of Northern Ireland's history – the current Troubles having begun in 1968 – *The Táin* seemed to speak not so much of an ancient past, but of an urgent present. Like many others of my generation, I well remember the shock and delight I experienced when I first read it.

The present translation would not have been possible without Kinsella's ground-breaking text. Had Kinsella not undertaken his translation, there would have been no public consciousness of *Táin Bó Cúailnge*. As I write, my original copy of the Oxford paperback edition of 1970 is on my desk, as it has been throughout the process of my translation. I began by trying not to compare my efforts with his; but I found the temptation to peep irresistible and, thereafter, as I proceeded with the translation, I checked every line of mine against Kinsella. I trust my translation is different. Nevertheless, there are occasions when my words do not differ a great deal from his. That is inevitable when more than one translation emerges from more or less the same text. And for better or for worse, my translation will be seen as a commentary on Kinsella; I hope it will also be taken as a tribute.

My sources for the original text are Cecile O'Rahilly's editions, *Táin Bó Cúailnge from the Book of Leinster*, and *Táin Bó Cúailnge Recension I* (Dublin, 1967 and 1976). A list of translations consulted appears in the 'Further Reading' section. I have followed Kinsella in taking Recension I as my base text, but I have ordered some of the episodes somewhat differently, and included some doublets and apparent contradictions that he has left out. Like him, I have incorporated elements of the 'Book of Leinster' text, notably the pillow-talk and the Fer Diad episodes; I have also included some short passages that he has not. It should be noted that both recensions are divided into numerous headed sections – 'The Death of Órlám', 'The Death of Lethan', 'The Combat of Fer Diad and Cú Chulainn', and so forth. Recension I has fifty-two such episodes, varying in length from a few lines to several pages. Such an arrangement might be used to support the theory that the *Táin* is a source-book rather than a consistent, chronological narrative. Like Kinsella, I have ignored these divisions and their headings for the sake of narrative flow, and have arranged the translation in thirteen 'chapters' (Kinsella has fourteen).

Kinsella's *Táin* is prefaced by seven *remscéla* (prefatory tales or 'prequels') which gave a background to the main narrative. I have not included these, but summarize them, where relevant, in the Notes to the text. Like Kinsella, I have attempted in the prose passages to be as faithful as possible to the Old Irish, if not wholly literal, and I trust that my translation can always be justified against the original. Kinsella, in his Introduction, acknowledges that it was necessary to take some liberties with the verse, and more particularly with the *rosc* passages: I do the same, but my treatment differs significantly from his in some respects. Firstly, I wanted to preserve in the translation some of the formal aspects of the poems. Whereas Kinsella renders these as relatively free verse, I have kept to the original syllable-count of the lines, except in a very few instances where it proved impossible. I have also included rhyme and assonance, though not in the manner of the original, since the *aabb* pattern of much of the verse would be difficult and tedious to replicate in English. Secondly, I have rendered the *rosc* passages into a kind of prose poetry which, by leaving gaps between phrases, attempts to indicate some of the syntactical ambiguity of the original. Overall, I hope I have given some notion of the stylistic heterogeneity of the text.

With regard to place-names and personal names, I have retained the Old Irish spellings more or less as they are in O'Rahilly's text. A guide to their pronunciation follows this section. The Irish names are rarely without meaning, and, for an Old Irish audience, would have acted as a kind of ironic commentary on the action. For instance, one of Cú Chulainn's many ill-advised opponents is called Fer Báeth, which translates literally as 'foolish man'. I have followed Kinsella's practice in giving English equivalents for some of the names within the text, and have done so in rather more instances, but only when it was possible to do so without disturbing the flow of the narrative. In other cases, where plausible equivalents can be found (and many of the names resist translation), they are glossed in the Notes to the text. Some of my derivations are speculative, or may be the product of wishful thinking; but this is wholly in the spirit of the *dindsenchas* tradition of fanciful etymology, not to mention the tendency of the *Táin* authors to invent place-names to fit the record. Likewise, my amalgamation and re-ordering of the original materials reflects the *Táin*'s history of being rewritten and edited by various hands. There is no canonical *Táin*, and every translation of it is necessarily another version or recension.

## NOTES

1.  In 1973 the concept of the *Táin* was brought to an even larger audience when the 'Celtic rock' group Horslips released an album of the same name, with songs and music inspired by the Kinsella translation.
2.  A point made in Maria Tymoczo, *Translation in a Postcolonial Context* (Manchester: 1999).

# Pronunciation Guide

Old Irish orthography is governed by complex rules and the following is intended only as an approximate and very simplified guide.

## Consonants

Initial consonants are pronounced approximately as in English. C is always hard: when followed by a, o, or u it is pronounced as in English 'cup'; when followed by e or i, it is pronounced as in English 'cap'. Final d and g are occasionally silent. Elsewhere, consonants are generally as follows:

b = v
c = g
ch is guttural, as in Scottish 'loch'
d = *dh*, as in English 'then', represented in the Examples by ð
g = *gh*, a soft guttural, like a gargled ch
m = v, except for Fedelm and Leborcham
t = d
s followed or preceded by e or i = sh
th = *th*, as in 'thin', represented in the Examples by θ

# Vowels

a = as in English 'pat'
e = as in 'pet'
i = as in 'pit'
o = as in 'pot'
u = as in 'putt'

Final e is always sounded.

Long vowels, marked with an accent, á, é, í, ó, ú, are pronounced awe, ay, ee, owe, oo.

# Examples

Stressed syllables in bold. Guttural ch is represented by ċ, guttural g as ġ

*Persons*

Ailill: **a**lill
Amargin: **a**varġin
Badb: baiv
Bricriu: **brick**ru
Cathbad: **kaff**a
Conchobar: **con**covir
Cormac: **cor**mok
Deichtire: **deċ**tir-e
Dubthach: **duff**ach
Emer: **ay**ver
Etarcomol: **e**darkovol
Eochaid: **owċ**ee
Eogan: **owġ**an
Fedelm: **feð**elm
Ferdia: fer**dee**-a

*Places etc.*

Áth Ferdia: **awθ** ir**dee**-a
Áth Gabla: **awθ** gavla
Brug: broo
Conaille: **con**il-eh
Crúachan Aí: **croo**-aċan ee
Cúailnge: **cool**ing-e
Cluain: **clew**-in
Dub: duv
Dún Sobairche: **doon sov**irċ-e
Emain Macha: **evin maċ**a
Fid: fee
Mag: maġ
Méithe: **may**θ-e
Midi: **mið**i
Mórthruaille: more-**θrool**-yeh

*Persons*

Fergus Mac Róich: **ferġus mok
roy**
Finnabair: **fin**avir
Follomain: **follo**vin
Laeg: **loyġ**
Leborcham: **levorċam**
Laeghaire: **loyġeh**-re
Maine: **ma**-ne
Medb: mayv
Morrígan: **moreeġan**
Nemain: **nevin**
Noisiu: **noyshu**
Scáthach: **scawθach**
Sétanta: **shay**danda
Sualdam: **soo**-aldav

*Places etc.*

Muirthemne: **mur**hevn-e
Sechaire: **sheċir**-e
Slaiss: shlish
Slechta: **shleċta**
Sliab Fuait: **shlee**-av **foo**-id
Táin: toyn
Tethba: **teffa**

# I
# THE
# PILLOW TALK
# AND ITS
# OUTCOME

ONE NIGHT WHEN the royal bed had
been prepared for Ailill[1] and Medb[2] in Crúachan[3] Fort in
Connacht, they engaged in pillow-talk:

'It's true what they say, girl,' said Ailill. 'Well-off woman,
wealthy man's wife.'

'True enough,' said the woman. 'What makes you say it?'

'Just this,' said Ailill, 'that you're better off now than the
day I took you.'

'I was well-off before it,' said Medb.

'If you were, I never heard tell of it,' said Ailill, 'apart
from your woman's assets that your neighbour enemies kept
plundering and raiding.'

'Not so,' said Medb, 'for my father was High King of
Ireland – namely, Eochu Feidlech son of Finn son of Finnoman
son of Finnen son of Fingall son of Roth son of Rigéon son
of Blathacht son of Beothacht son of Enna Agnech son of
Angus Turbech. He had six daughters: Derbriu, Ethne, Éle,
Clothru, Muguin, Medb. I was the noblest and most cele-
brated of them all. The most generous in bestowing gifts and
favours. The best at warfare, strife and combat. I had fifteen
hundred royal mercenaries, the sons of exiles, and as many
more the sons of freeborn native men, and for every soldier
of them I had ten, and for every ten I had nine more, and
eight, and seven, and six, and five, and four, and three, and
two, and one.[4] And that was just my household guard.

'Then my father gave me a province of Ireland, Connacht

that is ruled from Crúachan. That is why I am called Medb of Crúachan. Envoys came from Finn the King of Leinster, the son of Ross Ruad, to woo me, and from Cairbre the son of Niafer King of Tara – another son of Ross Ruad – and from Conchobar[5] King of Ulster, son of Fachtna, and from Eochaid Bec. I turned them all down. I asked a more exacting wedding-gift than any woman ever before me – a man without meanness, jealousy and fear.

'If he were mean, we'd be ill-matched, because I am generous in bestowing gifts and favours. And it would be a disgrace if I were more generous than him, but no disgrace if we are equal, both bestowing freely. If he were cowardly, we'd be ill-matched, for I am powerful in warfare, fight and fray. It would be a disgrace if I were more forcible than him, but no disgrace if both of us are forcible. Nor would it do for my husband to be jealous: I never had one man without another waiting in his shadow. I got the right man – yourself, Ailill, the other son of Ross Ruad of Leinster. You are not mean, you are not jealous, you are not cowardly. When we made the contract, I gave you a bride-price that befits a woman: outfits for a dozen men, a chariot worth thrice seven bondmaids, the breadth of your face in red gold, the weight of your left arm in white bronze. Whoever brings you shame or strife or trouble, you've no claim to compensation or redress, beyond what I claim, for you're a man dependent on a woman's wealth.'

'Not so,' said Ailill, 'for I have two brothers, Cairbre who rules Tara, and Finn the King of Leinster. And I let them rule because of seniority, not because they were more generous with their largesse. I never heard of a province of Ireland that depended on a woman's assets except this one, which is why I came and assumed the throne in succession to my mother, for she is Máta Muiresc, Mágach's daughter. And what better queen for me, than the daughter of the High King of Ireland?'

'All the same,' said Medb, 'my wealth is greater than yours.'

'You astonish me,' said Ailill. 'No one has more wealth, more goods and jewels than myself. I know this for a fact.'

So the least valuable of their assets were brought out, to see who had more wealth and goods and jewels: their cauldrons and buckets and pots, their porringers and tubs and basins. Then their gold artefacts, their rings and their bracelets and their thumb-rings were brought out, and their outfits of purple and blue and black and green and yellow, whether plain or multi-coloured, plaid, checked or striped. Their flocks of sheep were brought in from the fields and the meadows and the green lawns. They were counted and compared, and found to be equal in number and size. Among Medb's sheep was a prize ram worth one bondmaid, and among Ailill's was one to match.

From pasture and paddock and stable their horses and steeds were brought in. Among Medb's horses was a prize stallion worth one bondmaid, and Ailill had one to match. Their great herds of swine were brought in from the woods and the glens and the wastelands. They were reckoned and counted and claimed, and found to be equal in size and number. Medb had a prize boar, and Ailill had another.

Then their herds of cows and droves of cattle were brought in from the woods and the wastes of the province. They were reckoned and counted and claimed, and found to be equal in size and number. But among Ailill's cattle was a prize bull, that had been a calf of one of Medb's cows – Finnbennach his name, the White-horned. Not wanting to be reckoned as a woman's asset, he had gone over to the king's herd. And to Medb it was as if she hadn't a single penny, for there was no bull to equal Finnbennach among her cattle.

Mac Roth the Messenger[6] was summoned by Medb, and Medb told Mac Roth to go and see if the match of the bull might be found in any of the provinces of Ireland.

'I know where to find such a bull and better,' said Mac Roth, 'in the province of Ulster in the district of Cúailnge[7] in the house of Dáire Mac Fiachna. His name is the Donn[8] Cúailnge, the Brown Bull of Cúailnge.'

'Take yourself there, Mac Roth,' said Medb, 'and ask Dáire

for a year's loan of the Donn Cúailnge, and when the year is
up I'll give him back the Brown Bull and fifty heifers to boot.
And you can make him another offer, Mac Roth. If the people
of those borderlands begrudge the loan of the Pride of the
Herd, the Donn Cúailnge, let Dáire himself bring me the bull
and I'll grant him a piece of the smooth plain of Aí as big as
all his lands, and a chariot worth thrice seven bondmaids,
as well as the friendship of my own thighs.'

Messengers set out for Dáire Mac Fiachna's house. There
were nine of them in Mac Roth's band. Mac Roth was made
welcome in Dáire's house, as was right and proper for a Head
Messenger. Dáire asked him what had brought him on his
journey, and why he had come. The Messenger told him why
he had come, and of the dispute between Medb and Ailill.

'So I've come to ask for the loan of the Donn Cúailnge,' he
said, 'to match the White-horned Bull. And when the loan is
up, you'll get back the Brown Bull and fifty heifers into the
bargain. And there's more on offer: if you bring the bull
yourself, you'll get a piece of the smooth plain of Aí as big as
all your lands, and a chariot worth thrice seven bondmaids,
as well as the friendship of Medb's thighs.'

Dáire was well pleased by this. He leaped up and down on
his couch and the seams of the flock mattress burst beneath him.

' 'Pon my soul!' he cried. 'Let the Ulstermen say what they
will, I'll take the Pride of the Herd, the Donn Cúailnge, to
Ailill and Medb in the land of Connacht.'

Mac Roth was well pleased by Dáire's response.

The messengers were attended to, and straw and fresh
rushes strewn for them. They were given a feed of meat and
drink, until they were well full. Two of the messengers'
tongues got loose.

'It's true what they say,' said one, 'that the man of this
house is a great man.'

'Very true,' said the other.

'Is there a better man in Ulster?' said the first messenger.

'There is indeed,' said the second messenger. 'Dáire's

master, Conchobar, is a better man, for if every man in Ulster bowed to him, there'd be no shame on them. Mind you, it was very great of Dáire to give us nine foot-soldiers what would have been a job for the four strong provinces of Ireland, that is, to bring the Donn Cúailnge out of Ulster.'

A third messenger joined the conversation.

'What's all the talk about?' he said.

'Your man here was saying that the man of this house is a great man. Very true, says your other man. Is there a better man in Ulster? says your man here. There is indeed, says your other man. Dáire's master, Conchobar, is a better man, for if every man in Ulster bowed to him, there'd be no shame on them. Mind you, it was very great of Dáire to give us nine foot-soldiers what would have been a job for the four strong provinces of Ireland, that is, to bring the Donn Cúailnge out of Ulster.'

'I'd like to see the mouth that said that spout blood, for if he hadn't given willingly, we would have taken the bull anyway.'

Just then Dáire Mac Fiachna's head butler came into their quarters with a man carrying drink and another food, and he heard what they were saying. In a fit of rage he put down the food and drink. And he didn't say, 'Help yourselves', and he didn't say, 'Don't help yourselves.' He went straight to Dáire Mac Fiachna's quarters, and said:

'Are you the man who gave the messengers the Pride of the Herd, the Donn Cúailnge?'

'I am indeed,' said Dáire.

'That's not the gesture of a king, for what they say is true, that if you hadn't given him willingly, he would have been taken anyway by the forces of Ailill and Medb, and the craftiness of Fergus Mac Róich.'[9]

'By the gods I worship, nothing will leave here without my leave!'

They waited until morning. The messengers were up early and they went to Dáire's quarters.

'Tell us, your lordship, where we might find the Donn Cúailnge.'

'Indeed I will not,' said Dáire, 'and if I were the sort of man to give foul play to any messenger or traveller or guest that comes this way, none of you would leave here alive.'

'Why's that?' said Mac Roth.

'There's a very good reason why,' said Dáire. 'You said that whatever I didn't give willingly, it would be taken from me anyway by the forces of Ailill and Medb, and the craftiness of Fergus Mac Róich.'

'Come now,' said Mac Roth, 'you shouldn't heed what messengers say when they've a feed of your meat and drink in them. It's not as if it was Ailill's and Medb's fault.'

'All the same, Mac Roth, I won't be giving up my bull.'

The messengers returned to Crúachan Fort in Connacht. Medb asked them for their news, and Mac Roth broke the news – that they had not brought back the bull from Dáire.

'Why not?' said Medb.

Mac Roth told her why not.

'There's no need to iron out the knots in this one, Mac Roth,' said Medb, 'for it was known that if the bull were not given willingly, he would be taken by force. And taken he shall be.'

# II
# THE
# TÁIN
# BEGINS

A GREAT ARMY was mustered in Connacht by Ailill and Medb, and a call to arms went out to the other three provinces. Ailill sent messengers to his six brothers, namely, Cet, Anlúan, Maccorb, Bascall, Én and Dóche, all sons of Mágach. Each brought three thousand men. And Ailill sent word to Cormac Conn Longas the Exile,[1] who was billeted in Connacht with his three thousand men.

Cormac's men marched to Crúachan in three divisions. The first division wore dappled cloaks. Their heads were shaved. They wore knee-length tunics. Each man was equipped with a long shield, a silver-handled sword and a broad bright spear on a slender shaft.

'Is that Cormac?' said they all.

'Not yet,' said Medb.

The second division wore dun-grey cloaks and calf-length tunics with red embroidery. Their long hair hung down their backs. Each man was equipped with a bright shield, swords with guards of gold and a five-pronged spear.

'Is that Cormac?' said they all.

'Not yet,' said Medb.

The third division arrived. They wore purple cloaks and hooded, ankle-length tunics with red embroidery. Their hair was cut shoulder-length. Each man was equipped with a curved, scallop-edged shield and a 'palace-turret' spear. Together they lifted their feet, and together they put them down again.

'Is that Cormac?' said they all.

'That's Cormac,' said Medb.

That night they pitched camp and thick smoke rose from their fires between the four fords of Aí – Moga, Bercna, Slissen and Coltna. They stayed there for a fortnight, drinking and feasting and revelling to ease the hardship of the imminent campaign. Then Medb asked her charioteer to hitch up the horses for her to go and consult her druid. She arrived at the druid's place and asked him to look into the future.

'There are those today who leave behind lovers, friends and relations. And if they do not come back safe and sound, they all will curse me, because I made the call to arms. Yet I too have to go, and count myself as much as them. Find out for me if I will come back or not.'

And the druid said: 'Whoever comes back or not, you will come back.'

The driver turned the chariot round. As they made to go back to camp a young woman appeared before them. She had yellow hair. She wore a dappled cloak with a gold pin, a hooded tunic with red embroidery and shoes with gold buckles. Her face was broad above and slender beneath, her eyebrows dark, and her black eyelashes cast a shadow halfway down her cheek. Her lips were of a Parthian red, inset with teeth like pearls. Her hair was done up in three plaits, two wound round her head and the third hanging down her back to her calf. In her hand was a weaver's beam of white bronze inlaid with gold. Her eyes had triple irises. The young woman was armed. Her chariot was drawn by two black horses.

'What is your name?' said Medb to the young woman.

'My name is Fedelm, one of the women poets of Connacht.'

'Where have you come from?' said Medb.

'From learning poetry in Alba,' said the young woman.

'Have you the Second Sight?' said Medb.

'I have that too,' said the young woman.

'Look for us, then, and see how our expedition will fare.'

The girl looked.

And Medb said: 'For our army, Fedelm, what lies ahead?'

Fedelm replied: 'I see it crimson, I see it red.'

'That can't be right,' said Medb, 'for Conchobar is in Emain, laid low by the Curse,[2] together with the rest of the Ulster warriors. My spies have told me so.'

And Medb said: 'For our army, Fedelm, what lies ahead?'

Fedelm replied: 'I see it crimson, I see it red.'

'That can't be right,' said Medb, 'for Conchobar Mac Uthidir is in Dún Lethglaise with a third of Ulster's forces, and Fergus son of Róich Mac Echdach and his force of three thousand are here with us in exile.'

And Medb said: 'For our army, Fedelm, what lies ahead?'

Fedelm replied: 'I see it crimson, I see it red.'

'That's neither here nor there,' said Medb. 'Whenever a great army musters, there is bound to be trouble and strife and bloody wounds. Soldiers will boast and soldiers will quarrel before the onset of any expedition. I want the truth.'

And Medb said: 'For our army, Fedelm, what lies ahead?'

Fedelm replied: 'I see it crimson, I see it red.'

Then the young woman chanted this verse:

> I see a forceful blond man,
> on whom victories are built.
> A fierce light springs from his head,
> wounds hang on him like a belt.

> Seven jewels play about
> the stark pupil of each eye.
> His sharp teeth are unsheathed.
> He wears a shirt of crimson dye.

> His features are beautiful,
> his form pleasing to women –
> deadly handsome and youthful,
> in battle like a dragon.

That same courage can be found
in the famous Blacksmith's Hound –
Cú Chulainn of Muirthemne.[3]
Who this is I do not know,
but this I know for certain –
he stains red his every foe.

I see him loom on the plain,
a whole army to withstand,
wielding four short, sharp, smart swords
in each of his two deft hands.

He attacks in battle-gear
with his fierce barbed *gae bolga*,[4]
his bone-hilted sword, his spear,
each picked for a special use.

Red-cloaked he drives through the field,
uttering a battle-hymn.
From his chariot he deals
death across the left wheel-rim,
the Torqued Man[5] changed terribly
from when his form first struck me.

He's taken the war-path now.
Havoc unless you pay heed
to Sualdam's son, the Hound.
He pursues you with all speed.

Acres will be dense with dead,
as he mows the battlefield,
leaving a thousand lopped heads:
these things I do not conceal.

Blood spurts from soldiers' bodies,
released by this hero's hand.
He kills on sight, scattering
Deda's followers and clan.[6]
Women wail at the corpse-mound
because of him – the Forge-Hound.

They set out the Monday after Samhain. This was their route,
south-east from Crúachan Aí:

through Mag Cruinn, the Round Plain,
through Tuaim Móna, the Mound of Turf,
through Turloch Teóra Crích, the Vanishing
     Lake of the Borderlands,
through Cúl Sílinne, the Dripping Backwater,
through Dubloch, the Black Lake,
through Fid Dubh, the Black Wood,
through Badbna,
through Coltain, the Feast,
across the Shannon,
through Glúine Gabur, the Goat's Knees,

through Mag Trega, the Plain of Spears,
through North Tethba,
through South Tethba,
through Cúl, the Backwater,
through Ocháin,
northwards through Uata,
southwards through Tiarthechta,
through Ord, the Hammer,
thorugh Slaiss, the Blows,
through Indeoin, the Anvil,

through Carn,
through Meath,
through Ortrach,

through Findglassa Assail, Assal's Clear Stream,
through Drong, the Tribe,
through Delt,
through Duelt,
through Deland,
through Selach,
through Slabra, the Chain,

through Slechta, the Cut, where they cut their way
    through,
through Cúl, the Backwater, of Siblinne,
by Dub, the Blackwater,
southwards through Ochon,
through Catha,
southwards through Cromma, the Crooked Plain,
through Tromma, the Heavy Plain,
eastwards through Fodromma,
through Sláine,
through Gort Sláine,

southwards through Druim Licce, the Flagstone
    Ridge,
through Áth Gabla, the Ford of the Fork,
through Ard Achad, the High Field,
northwards by Feorann, the Green Sward,
through Finnabair, the White Stream,
southwards through Assa,
through Airne,
through Aurthaile,
through Druim Salfind, the White-heeled Ridge,
through Druim Caín, the Fair Ridge,

through Druim Caimthechta, the Ridge of the
    Crooked Road,
through Druim MacDega,
through the Lesser Eo Dond, the Brown Yew,

through the Greater Eo Dond,
through Méide in Togmaill, the Stoat's Neck,
through Méide in Eoin, the Bird's Neck,
through Baile, the Town,
through Aille, the Cliffs,
through Dall Scena, the Knife's Blind Spot,
through Ball Scena, the Knife's Resting-place,

through Ross Mor, the Promontory,
through Scuap, the Broom,
through Imscuap, the Better Broom,
through Cenn Ferna, the Man's Head,
through Anmag, the Plain of Plains,
through Fid Mór, the Great Wood,
through Colbtha, the Yearlings,
by the River Cronn,
through Druim Caín on the road to Midluachair,
    Among the Rushes
to Finnabair in Cúailnge.

Such was the route they took.

# III

# THEY GET
# TO KNOW
# ABOUT
# CÚ CHULAINN

ON THE FIRST stage of their march they went from Crúachan to Cúl Sílinne, the site of Loch Carrcín today. Medb told her driver to hitch up her nine chariots for her to make a circuit of the camp, to see who was keen to be on the march, and who was not so keen.

Meanwhile Ailill's tent had been pitched, and fitted with beds and blankets. Next to Ailill was Fergus Mac Róich in his tent; next to Fergus, Cormac Conn Longas; next to him, Conall Cernach; and next to him, Fiacha Mac Fir Febe, the son of Conchobar's daughter. Medb, daughter of Eochaid Fedlech, was on Aillil's other side; next to her, their daughter Finnabair; next to her was Flidais. Not to mention underlings and servants.

Medb came back from inspecting the army and said it wouldn't do for them to proceed further if the three-thousand-strong division of the Gailéoin[1] were to go as well.

'Why do you disrespect them?' said Ailill.

'I don't disrespect them,' said Medb. 'They are excellent soldiers. While the others were just getting round to building their huts, they had thatched theirs, and were busy cooking. While the others were beginning to eat, they had finished, and their harpers were playing for them. So it won't do for them to come. They'd take all the credit for our army's triumph.'

'But they're on our side,' said Ailill.

'They can't come,' said Medb.

'Let them stay, then,' said Ailill.

'They can't stay,' said Medb, 'for by the time we've come back, they'll have seized all our lands.'

'What's to be done with them, then,' said Ailill, 'since neither their coming nor their staying pleases you?'

'Wipe them out,' said Medb.

'A typical woman's ploy, I have to say,' said Ailill.

'And it won't happen,' said Fergus, 'unless you wipe out all of us, for the Gailéoin are allies of us Ulster exiles.'

'That could be arranged,' said Medb. 'I have here my household guard of two divisions, each three thousand strong, and my sons the seven Maines are here, with their seven divisions, lucky as they are in battle. There's Maine Máithramail the Motherlike, Maine Athramail the Fatherlike, Maine Mórgor the Loyal Man, Maine Míngor the Loyal Boy, Maine Móepirt the Incomparable, whom some call Maine Milscothach the Sweet Talker, Maine Andoe the Quick Man, and Maine Cotagaib Uile, the Man of All Qualities, who is the image of both his father and his mother, and who bears himself as proudly.'

'There's more to it than that,' said Fergus. 'For we have seven kings of Munster here, each with his division of three thousand. And I could take you on right now, in this camp, my own division helped by those seven divisions, not to mention the three thousand Gailéoin. But let's not go into that,' said Fergus. 'We can arrange things so that the Gailéoin will prove no threat to the main force. We have seventeen divisions encamped here, three thousand in each division, not counting camp followers, and children, and women, for each king in Medb's company has brought his consort. The Gailéoin make up the eighteenth division. Let them be split up among the whole army.'

'Whatever it takes,' said Medb, 'provided they don't stay in the close ranks they form now.'

So it was done. The Gailéoin were split up among the whole army, so that no five of them remained together.

Next morning they set off towards Móin Coltna, the Banquet Bog. They came across eight score deer in a single herd.

They encircled them and killed them. Wherever there was a Gailéoin soldier, he got a deer. The rest of the army got five deer between them. Then they came to Mag Trega, the Plain of Spears, where they camped and prepared their food. Some people say that it was here that Dubthach² chanted this verse:

Listen well to Dubthach's words
uttered in a dream of strife –
armies gearing up because
the White Horn left Ailill's wife.

One man equal to a force
protects Muirthemne's cattle.
Since two swineherds once were friends,³
crows drink the milk of battle.

The dark waters of the Cronn
will keep them from Muirthemne,
until soldier's work be done
up North at Mount Ochaíne.

Quick, says Ailill to Cormac,
come and stand by your son's side.
Cattle graze upon the plain,
battle-din spreads far and wide.

War will come when it is due
with a third of Medb's forces.
Should the Torqued Man come to you
he'll make dead meat of you all.

Then the Nemain – the Battle Goddess⁴ – assailed them. It was not the quietest of nights for them, for Dubthach kept bawling out in his sleep. Many started from their beds, and panic swept through the ranks until Medb came forth and restored order.

*

The army marched on. They discussed who should lead them
from one province to the other, and it was agreed it should
be Fergus, because this, for him, was a grudge war: he had
been King of Ulster for seven years, and when the sons of
Usnech had been put to death despite his guarantees, he had left
the province, and had been seventeen years away from Ulster
in enmity and exile. So it seemed right that Fergus should be
their leader. Fergus led them, but he still felt pangs of affection
for the people of his native province, and he led the troops
astray, making a great detour to the south; and he sent messengers to warn the Ulstermen, and employed a series of delaying
tactics. Ailill and Medb noticed this, and Medb said:

> Fergus, this is a strange way.
> Do we go back or forward?
> To the north and south we stray
> through every kind of border.

Fergus replied:

> Medb, what disorders you so?
> There's no double-crossing here.
> Woman, we need to go slow
> to the Ulstermen's empire.

Medb said:

> Ailill and I were afraid
> that you'd played the army false.
> Or perhaps your mind has strayed
> from taking the proper course?

Fergus replied:

> The crooked way that I went
> was not to betray our men

but rather to circumvent
the Guard of Muirthemne Plain.

Medb said:

If you are swayed by kinship,
don't you think you should abstain
from leading horses? Perhaps
someone else should take the reins.

Fergus replied:

My mind has not gone astray
from homesickness. I just mean
to put off the certain day
when we shall meet Cú Chulainn.

After the army had been led astray over bogland and
border, they went to Granard in North Tebtha, where they
spent the night. Meanwhile Fergus's warning messages had
been received by the Ulstermen, who were still laid low by the
Curse, all except Cú Chulainn and his father Sualdam. When
they got Fergus's message they went as far as Ard Cuillenn,
the Holly Height, to watch for the enemy forces. Their horses
grazed around the pillar-stone that stands there. Sualdam's
horses cropped the grass down to the soil on the north side,
and Cú Chulainn's horses cropped the grass down to the soil
and the bedrock on the south side.

'Father, I feel it in my bones,' said Cú Chulainn, 'that the
enemy is near. Go and warn the Ulstermen not to stay on the
open plains, but to keep to the woods and the wastelands
and the wild glens of the province so as to evade the Irish
army.'

'And you, my son, where will you go?'

'I must go south to Tara, to meet Fedelm Nóichroide'
– some people say he meant to spend the night with her

bondmaid, who was secretly his bedfellow – 'to fulfil a solemn promise I made to her.'

'Shame on anyone who does so,' said Sualdam, 'and leaves the Ulstermen to be ground underfoot by their enemies, for the sake of going to see a woman.'

'But I must go, for if I don't, men's promises will be called lies, and women's promises the truth.'

Sualdam went to warn the Ulstermen. Cú Chulainn went into the wood and with a single stroke he cut a prime oak sapling. Closing one eye, and using one foot and one hand, he made a hoop of it. He cut an ogam[5] inscription on the peg of the hoop, and he put the hoop around the narrow part of the standing stone of Ard Cuillenn, and he forced the hoop down on to the thick part of the stone. Then he went on to see his woman.

The Irish army approached Ard Cuillenn. Eirr and Innel and their two charioteers Foich and Fochlam[6] – the four sons of Iraird Mac Anchinne – were at the head of the army. It was their job to keep the cloaks and rugs and brooches of the main force from being soiled by the dust raised up as they advanced. They found the hoop left there by Cú Chulainn, and noticed how Sualdam's horses had cropped the grass down to the soil, while Cú Chulainn's had cropped it down to the bedrock. They sat and waited till the main force came up, and their harpers played for them. They gave the hoop to Fergus Mac Róich, who read out the ogam inscription on it.

When Medb arrived she said:

'Why are you waiting here?'

'We're waiting,' said Fergus, 'because of this hoop. There's an ogam message on its peg, which reads, "Proceed no further, unless a man among you can make a hoop like this from one tree with one hand. Anyone except my comrade Fergus." Obviously, Cú Chulainn has done this. It was his horses that grazed here.'

He gave the hoop to a druid and chanted this verse:

This hoop: what does it imply?
What is its secret intent?
And how many put it here?
One man? Or a regiment?

Will havoc strike our forces
if we overstep this mark?
Druids, explain if you can
these words cut into the bark.

The druid replied:

A great soldier cut this hoop
to confound his enemies
and contain a royal troop –
just one man, with just one hand.

The king's army must obey
or transgress the rule of war,
unless one of you finds a way
to do what one has done.
That is all I know of why
the hoop was left on the stone.

Then Fergus said:

'If you ignore this hoop and go past it, I swear that the great soldier who made it will find you, though you be hidden underground or in a locked room, and he will kill one of you before morning, unless you make a hoop just as he did.'

'We are not so eager for one of our men to be killed just yet,' said Ailill. 'Let's make our way through the wood to the south of us, Fid Dúin. We don't need to go this way.'

The army cut down the wood to make a road for the chariots. The place is called Slechta, the Cut.

According to another account, however, it was here that the colloquy between Medb and the Prophetess Fedelm took place, as related above; and the wood was cut down after an answer she gave to Medb, thus:

'Look for me,' said Medb, 'and see how my army will do.'

'It is hard for me,' said the young woman. 'I can't see them properly for the wood.'

'We'll soon change that,' said Medb. 'We'll cut down the wood.'

So it was done, and Slechta is the name of that place. The Cut.

It is here that the Partraigi[7] dwell.

They spent the night in Cúil Sibrille – Cennannas,[8] as it is now known. A heavy snow fell on them, up to the men's belts and the chariot-wheels. They could prepare no food nor could they sleep, and they rose early to make their way across the glistening snow.

As for Cú Chulainn, it wasn't so early when he got up after spending the night with his woman. Then he had to wash and bathe, and it was later still when he told his charioteer, Láeg,[9] to hitch up the horses. Eventually they found the tracks of the army.

'If only we hadn't gone there,' said Cú Chulainn, 'and betrayed the men of Ulster. We've let the army come through and gave no warning. Make an estimate of the enemy's numbers.'

Láeg examined the tracks from all sides, and said to Cú Chulainn:

'They're all mixed up. I can't arrive at an estimate.'

'They wouldn't be mixed up if I looked at them,' said Cú Chulainn.

'Get out of the chariot,' said Láeg.

Cú Chulainn got out of the chariot and examined the tracks for a long time.

'Even you don't find it easy,' said Láeg.

'It is easier for me, however,' said Cú Chulainn, 'for I have three gifts – namely, the gift of sight, the gift of intellect and the gift of reckoning. I've reckoned up the numbers. There are eighteen divisions, each three thousand strong, but the eighteenth division – the three thousand Gailéoin – has been split up among the whole army, and that's what mixed up the count.'

Then Cú Chulainn made a detour around the army, till he came to Áth Grena, the Sunny Ford. He cut the fork of a tree with one stroke of his sword. He cut an ogam message on it and stuck it in the middle of the stream, so that a chariot could not pass on this side or that. No sooner done, than Eirr and Innel and their two charioteers Foich and Fochlam came upon him. He cut off their four heads and impaled them on the four prongs of the fork.

The horses of the four men went back to the army with their reins trailing and their harness covered in blood. Everyone thought they must have met a battle-force at the ford. A scouting party was sent ahead to see what had happened, but they saw nothing but the track of a single chariot and the fork with the four heads and the ogam inscription on it. Then the whole army came up.

'Are those the heads of some of our people?' said Medb.

'They are indeed, and some of our best people at that,' said Ailill.

One of the men read out the ogam writing on the side of the fork:

'One man stuck this fork here with one hand, and none shall pass it unless one of you pluck it out with one hand.'

'I'm astonished,' said Ailill, 'at how quickly the four were killed.'

'You should be more astonished,' said Fergus, 'that the fork was struck from the trunk with a single stroke, as will be seen by the single cut at its base, for it was planted without a hole being dug for it, and thrown with one hand from the back of a chariot.'

'Fergus, get us out of this fix,' said Medb.

'Bring me a chariot,' said Fergus.

They brought Fergus a chariot. He tugged at the fork with all his might, and the chariot broke into bits under him.

'Bring me another chariot,' said Fergus.

Again he tugged at the fork, and again the chariot broke into bits under him.

He broke seventeen of the Connachtmen's chariots in this way. Then he said:

'Bring me my own chariot.'

From his own chariot he pulled the fork from where it had been planted, and they saw that its base was a single cut.

Then Fergus chanted this verse:

Here is the famous forked pole
the hard man Cú Chulainn spiked
with the lopped heads of four foes
posted as a sign of spite.

Before none however brave
would he retreat from the fork.
The Hound left with limbs unscathed
and blood dripping from the bark.

Woe to the troops that march east
to hunt the rugged Brown Bull.
Men will be cut to pieces
by the fierce sword of the Hound.

Difficult to take the Bull
in battle with weapons keen.
When a thousand heads have rolled
Ireland and her tribes will weep.

Nothing more shall I say now
concerning Dechtire's son,[10]
but the business of the fork
shall be heard by everyone.

'What's the name of this ford, Fergus?' said Ailill.

'Áth Grena,' said Fergus, 'the Sunny Ford. But from now on it will be called Áth Gabla, the Ford of the Fork.'

# IV
# THE
# BOYHOOD
# DEEDS OF
# CÚ CHULAINN

'LET US TURN our minds,' said Ailill, 'to the kind of people we will soon have to deal with. Let you all make ready your food. It wasn't easy for you last night with the snow. And let us hear some of the adventures and stories of those people.'

It was then that they were told of the exploits of Cú Chulainn.

Ailill asked:

'Was it Conchobar who did this?'

'Not likely,' said Fergus. 'He'd never venture to the border country without a full battalion round him.'

'So, was it Celtchar Mac Uthidir?'[1]

'Not likely,' said Fergus. 'He'd never venture to the border country without a full battalion, either.'

'So, was it Eogan Mac Durthacht?'[2]

'Not likely. He'd never venture to the border country without thirty scythed chariots along with him. The candidate for this deed,' said Fergus, 'is Cú Chulainn. Only he would have cut the tree from its base with a single stroke, and killed the four as quickly as they were killed, and only he would have come to the border accompanied only by his charioteer.'

'What kind of man,' said Ailill, 'is this Hound of Ulster we hear tell of? How old is this notorious youth?'

'Not hard to tell,' said Fergus. 'In his fifth year he joined the games of the young fellows in Emain.[3] In his sixth year he went to study warcraft and tactics under Scáthach, the

Shadow, and to court Emer.[4] In his seventh year he took up
arms. He is now in his seventeenth year.'

'Is he the hardest man in Ulster?' said Medb.

'The hardest, surely,' said Fergus. 'You'll not meet a tougher
opponent – no spear-point sharper, quicker or more piercing;
no fighter fiercer, no raven more ravenous, no one of his age
a third as brave, no lion more ferocious; no bulwark in battle,
no mighty sledgehammer, no shield of soldiers, no nemesis of
armies, as able as him. There's no one of his generation to
match him for build, for gear, for fearsome looks or sweetness
of expression; none to match his splendid form and voice,
his stern strength, his striking-power and battle-bravery, his
doom-dealing fire and fury and his violence in victory, his skill
in stalking and slaughtering game, his swiftness, sureness and
unconquerable rage, not to mention the feat of nine men on
every spear-point – no, there's none to match Cú Chulainn.'

'Let's not pay too much heed to that,' said Medb. 'He has
only one body. He is mortal. He is not beyond capture.
Besides, he's only the age of a big girl, and his manly deeds
are yet to come.'

'Not so,' said Fergus. 'It would be little wonder for him to
perform great deeds right now, for even when he was a mere
boy, his deeds were those of a grown man.'

'He was reared,' said Fergus, 'by his father and mother at
Dairgdig, the Oaken House, in Muirthemne Plain. There he
heard great stories about the young fellows in Emain. At any
one time,' said Fergus, 'three fifties of young fellows there are
engaged in sport. This is how Conchobar spends his time ever
since he became king: one third of the day watching the young
fellows, one third playing chess,[5] and one third drinking ale
till he falls asleep while his musicians play for him. And
though he drove me into exile,' said Fergus, 'I'd still maintain
that he's the greatest warrior in Ireland.

'Cú Chulainn asked his mother to let him go and join the
young fellows.

' "You'll not go," said his mother, "without a bodyguard of Ulstermen."

' "I can't wait for them," said Cú Chulainn. "Point me towards Emain."

' "It's north from here," said his mother, "but it's hard travelling, for the heights of Sliab Fúait[6] lie between."

' "I'll try it, all the same," said Cú Chulainn.

'He set off with his toy shield and his toy javelin and his hurley-stick[7] and ball, and to shorten the journey he'd strike the ball a long way with his stick, then throw the stick after the ball, and the javelin after ball and stick. Then he would run after them and catch stick, ball and javelin before they hit the ground.

'He arrived at the great playing-field in Emain where the young fellows were playing a match, refereed by Follomain,[8] Conchobar's son. He ran on to the field and when the ball was struck towards him he caught it between his knees and not one of the boys managed to tackle him before he had carried the ball over the goal-line.

' "Well, boys," said Follomain, "have a go at yon fellow, for it's against the rules for another fellow to join the game without asking for permission or protection."

'Cú Chulainn didn't know that this was the form, that no one took the field without asking for permission or protection.

' "The fellow insults us," said Follomain, "though he does seem to be an Ulster fellow. Go for him!"

'They threw three fifties of javelins at him and they all stuck in his toy shield. They drove three fifties of hurling-balls at him and he stopped them all with his chest. They flung three fifties of hurleys at him, and he warded them off with his one hurley.

'The Torque seized him. His hair stood on end: you'd think each hair had been hammered into his head. Each hair seemed tipped with a spark, so sharply did they shoot upright. He closed one eye as narrow as the eye of a needle; he opened the other as wide as the mouth of a goblet. He bared his teeth from ear to ear. He opened his gob so wide you could see the inside of his gullet. The hero's light sprang from the crown of his head.

'Then he went for the young fellows. He knocked down fifty of them before they reached the gates of Emain. Nine of them,' said Fergus, 'clattered past Conchobar and myself as we were playing chess, and he came buck-lepping after them over the chess-board. Conchobar caught him by the wrist.

' "You're not treating these lads very well," said Conchobar.

' "I'm right not to, comrade Conchobar," he said. "I left my home, my mother and my father, to join their games, and they didn't treat me very well."

' "What's your name?" said Conchobar.

' "I am Sétanta[9] the son of Sualdam and your sister Dechtire. It didn't seem likely that I'd be attacked here."

' "Why didn't you get someone to protect you against the young fellows?"

' "I didn't know I had to. So give me your protection."

' "Agreed," said Conchobar.

'He turned round and began chasing through the house after the squad of young fellows.

' "What have you got in for them now?" said Conchobar.

' "I'm going to give them my protection," said Cú Chulainn.

' "Give it here and now," said Conchobar.

' "Agreed," said Cú Chulainn.

'Everyone went out to the playing field. And the boys who'd been knocked down got up again, helped by their foster-mothers and their foster-fathers.'

'For a while,' said Fergus, 'when he was just a lad in Emain, he couldn't get to sleep until morning.

' "Tell me," said Conchobar, "why you can't sleep."

' "I can't sleep unless my head and my feet are on the one level."

'So Conchobar had a stone plinth made for his head, and another for his feet, with a special bed propped between them.

'One time, some man or other went to wake him. Cú Chulainn hit him so hard on the forehead with his fist that he drove the bone into his brain, and knocked over the stone plinth with his arm.'

'Now that,' said Ailill, 'was a fighter's fist, and a champion's arm.'

'From then on,' said Fergus, 'no one dared wake him, but left him to wake in his own time.'

'Another time he was playing ball in the East Field, just himself against three fifties of young fellows. He kept beating them. They tried to grab hold of him but he laid into them with his fist and knocked out fifty of them. Then he showed them a clean pair of heels and hid under the mattress of Conchobar's bed. The whole of Ulster went for him. Conchobar went for him. I went for him myself. He got to his feet under the bed and he tossed the bed, and the thirty brave fellows that were hanging on to it, into the middle of the house. At length the Ulstermen cornered him. We got to talking then,' said Fergus, 'and made a peace between the young fellows and himself.'

'A war broke out between Ulster and Eogan Mac Durthacht. The Ulstermen went off to battle. Cú Chulainn was left to his sleep. Ulster got beat. Conchobar and Cúscraid Menn Macha and a pile of others were left for dead. Their groans awoke Cú Chulainn. He stretched himself and split the stone plinths at his head and feet. Bricriu[10] there saw it being done,' said Fergus. 'Then he got up. I saw him at the gate of the fort as I came in badly wounded.

'"Phew! Comrade Fergus! Good to see you!" he said. "Where's Conchobar?"

'"I don't know," I said.

'He went on his way. It was one dark night. He made for the battlefield. He met a man with half his head gone, and the half of another man on his back.

'"Help me, Cú Chulainn," he said. "I'm wounded and

I'm carrying half my brother on my back. Carry him a while for me."

'"I will not," said Cú Chulainn.

'The other threw his burden at him. Cú Chulainn threw it off. They grappled. Cú Chulainn was thrown down. Then I heard a thing – the Badb[11] calling out from among the corpses:

'"Poor material for a soldier, sprawled at the feet of a ghost!"

'Cú Chulainn got up, struck off his opponent's head with his hurley, and began driving it like a ball across the plain.

'"Is comrade Conchobar on the battlefield?"

'Conchobar made answer. Cú Chulainn went to him and found him in a ditch half-buried under a pile of muck.

'"What brings you to the battlefield," said Conchobar, "where you might catch your death of fright?"

'Cú Chulainn pulled him out of the ditch. No six of the strongest Ulstermen among us could have pulled him out so bravely.

'"Go on ahead to yonder house," said Conchobar, "and light me a fire."

'He lit a big fire for him.

'"Good," said Conchobar. "Now, if only I had a roast pig, I might just live."

'"I'll go and get one," said Cú Chulainn.

'He went out. He saw a man at a cooking-pit in the middle of the wood. One hand was on his weapons and the other was roasting a wild pig. He was one ferocious-looking man. But Cú Chulainn attacked him and took his head as well as the pig.

'Conchobar ate the pig.

'"Let's go home," said Conchobar.

'They found Cúscraid, Conchobar's son, on the way. He was badly wounded. Cú Chulainn took him on his back. Then the three of them made for Emain Macha.'

'Another time, the Ulstermen were laid low by the Curse. The Curse,' said Fergus, 'does not affect our women or children, or anyone from outside Ulster; nor does it affect Cú Chulainn and his father. And no one dares shed the blood of an Ulsterman when he's in this condition, for if they did they would get the Curse too, or they'd waste away, or die young.

'A raiding-party of twenty-seven came from the Isles of Faíche and broke into the rear courtyard while we lay smitten by the Curse. The women of the fort began screaming. The young fellows out on the playing-field came running in when they heard their cries. But when they saw these dark-looking men they took to their heels, all except Cú Chulainn. He attacked them with sling-stone and hurley-stick. He killed nine of them and received fifty wounds in the process. Then they made off. Is it any wonder,' said Fergus, 'that someone who could do such deeds when he was not yet five should come to the border and cut off the heads of those four?'

'This boy is well known to us,' said Conall Cernach, 'not least because he was given to us to foster. Not long after what Fergus told you, he did another great deed.

'Culann the smith was planning a great feast for Conchobar, and he asked him not to bring too many guests, for he hadn't much in the way of land or property to provide a big spread, only what he had earned by the work of his hands and his tongs. So Conchobar set out with fifty chariot-loads of the highest and mightiest of his warriors. Before he went he visited the playing-field: it was his custom, whether leaving or returning, to go there for the young fellows to wish him well. He saw Cú Chulainn playing ball against three fifties of young fellows, and beating them. When they played the Hole Game, Cú Chulainn filled the hole with all his shots, every one of them unstoppable. When it came their turn to shoot, he saved all their shots single-handed; not a single ball went past him. When they played Wrestling, he threw all three fifties of them by himself, and no matter how many came at him, they couldn't throw him. When they played Strip Tag, he stripped them all stark naked, while they couldn't so much as take the pin out of his cloak.

'Conchobar thought it was a wonderful performance. He asked if Cú Chulainn would still so outdo them in ability when they came to be big men. They all agreed that he would. Conchobar said to Cú Chulainn:

'"Come with me," he said, "to this great feast we're going to. I'd like you to be my guest."

'"I haven't finished playing yet, comrade Conchobar," said the lad. "I'll come on later."

'When everyone had arrived at the feast, Culann said to Conchobar:

'"Is there anyone else still to come?"

'"No one,' said Conchobar. He'd forgotten he'd invited his foster-son to join him.

'"I have a mastiff hound,' said Culann, "with three chains on him, and three men at the end of every chain. He's a Spanish breed. Let him loose to guard the livestock, and lock up the fort."

'Meanwhile the lad was approaching Culann's house. To shorten the way he'd throw his ball a long way, then, judging the distance exactly, he'd throw his hurley after the ball so that the hurley struck the ball. Then he'd run after them and catch ball and stick before they hit the ground. The hound got his scent and began to bay. Then it went for him. The lad struck his ball with his hurley so that the ball shot down the throat of the hound and carried its insides out through its backside. Then he grabbed two of its legs and smashed it to pieces against a nearby pillar-stone.

'Conchobar had heard the baying of the hound.

'"Ah, comrades," he said, "how I wish that this feast had never been!"

'"Why makes you say that?" they all asked.

'"The lad I invited to come later, my sister's son Sétanta, son of Sualdam, has been killed by the hound."

'All the Ulstermen jumped up and rushed out to fetch him, some of them leaping over the rampart, others through the gate. Fergus reached him first and carried him to Conchobar's arms. A great cheer went up, that the son of the king's sister had escaped death.

'Culann came out and saw his hound lying scattered in pieces.

'He went back into the house.

'"You are welcome, boy, for the sake of your mother's heart. But for my own part, how I wish that this feast had never been! My livelihood is no life, my household is an empty house, now that I have lost my hound. He guarded my life and my honour," he said, "this loyal servant that has been taken from me, my hound. He was shield and shelter for my goods and cattle, guardian of my beasts about the house or in the fields."

'"Not to worry," said the lad. "I'll rear you a pup of the same breed, and until such times as he's big and strong enough for work, I will be your hound to guard your cattle and yourself. And I will guard Muirthemne Plain; no herd or flock will be led away from me without my knowing it."

'"Then your name shall be Cú Chulainn, the Hound of Culann,"[12] said Cathbad.

'"It's a good name for me," said Cú Chulainn.

'It's no surprise that someone who did this when he was not yet seven should do great deeds now that he is seventeen,' said Conall Cernach.

'Here's another thing he did,' said Fiacha Mac Fir Febe. 'Cathbad the druid was staying with his son Conchobar Mac Nessa. Along with him were a hundred dedicated young men being trained in druid lore – those were the sort of numbers Cathbad would take on. One of his pupils asked him what that day might be favourable for. Cathbad said that if a warrior took up arms that day, his name would endure in Ireland as a byword for heroic deeds, and that stories about him would be told forever.

'Cú Chulainn heard this. He went to Conchobar to ask for arms, and Conchobor said:

'"On whose recommendation?"

'"Comrade Cathbad's," said Cú Chulainn.

'"We know Cathbad well,"[13] said Conchobar.

'He gave him sword, shield and spear. Cú Chulainn brandished them about the great hall and smashed them to bits. Conchobar gave him another sword, another shield, another spear. Cú Chulainn brandished them about the great hall and smashed them to bits. The lad went through the fifteen sets of weapons that Conchobar kept for novice warriors or in case of breakage, and he made bits and pieces of them all. Finally he was given Conchobar's own weapons. These did him rightly. He held them aloft and saluted the king whose arms they were, and said:

'"Long life to their kith and kin, whose king is the man whose arms these are!"

'Cathbad came in and said:

'"The boy is taking up arms?"

'"So," said Conchobar.

'"Then this is one unlucky mother's son," said Cathbad.

'"How's that? Did you not recommend him yourself?" said Conchobar.

'"Certainly not," said Cathbad.

'"Why did you lie to me, you twisted little imp?" said Conchobar to Cú Chulainn.

'"O King of the Fianna, it was no lie," said Cú Chulainn. "He was telling his pupils this morning, south of Emain, what this day might be favourable for, and I heard him, and that's why I came to you."

'"It is true," said Cathbad, "that this day favours one thing. There is no doubt that the one who takes up arms today will achieve great fame. But his life will be short."

'"Fine by me," said Cú Chulainn. "So long as I'm famous, I'm happy to live just one day on earth."

'Another day, someone else asked the druid what that day might be favourable for.

'"Whoever takes command of a chariot today," said Cathbad, "his name will live forever in Ireland."

'Cú Chulainn heard this, and went to Conchobar and said:

'"Comrade Conchobar, a chariot for me."

'A chariot was got for him. Cú Chulainn grabbed the shafts of the chariot, and broke the chariot. He broke twelve chariots in the same way. Finally, Conchobar's chariot was got for him, and it did him rightly. He got into the chariot with Conchobar's charioteer. The charioteer – he was called Ibor[14] – gave the chariot a turn.

'"You can get out now," said the charioteer. "These horses are very special."

'"I'm rather special myself, my good man," said Cú Chulainn. "Just drive on round Emain, and I'll make sure it's worth your while."

'The charioteer drove off and Cú Chulainn made him go down the road to greet the young fellows, "so as they can wish me luck". Then he had him go a bit further down the road, and as they drove on he said:

'"Don't spare the horses!"

'"Where to?" said Ibor.

'"Wherever the road takes us," said Cú Chulainn.

'So they came to Sliab Fúait, where they found Conall Cernach. It was Conall's turn to guard the province that day. Every one of Ulster's finest soldiers had a day-stint on Sliab Fúait, to offer safe passage to anyone who came with poetry, or challenge anyone who came to fight: no one proceeded to Emain without being checked.

'"May you prosper forever," said Conall, "and have victory in battle!"

'"Go back to the fort, Conall, and leave me here a while to stand guard," said Cú Chulainn.

'"You'd just about do," said Conall, "for taking care of someone who comes with poetry, but if it comes to fighting, you're a little young."

'"Let's leave it then," said Cú Chulainn. "Meanwhile, why don't we go and see what's happening down at the Loch

Echtra[15] crossing. There's usually a good gathering of warriors there."

' "Good choice," said Conall.

'They set off. Cú Chulainn fired a stone from his sling and broke the shaft of Conall's chariot.

' "Little boy, why did you fire that stone?" said Conall.

' "To test the accuracy of my hand and eye," said Cú Chulainn. "Now, comrade Conall, since it's against the Ulster code to drive a chariot which is unsafe, why don't you take yourself back to Emain, and leave me here to stand guard."

' "I've little choice," said Conall.

'So Conall Cernach went no further with him.

'Cú Chulainn went on to Loch Echtra but found no one there. The charioteer said to Cú Chulainn that they ought to get back to Emain in time for the drinking.

' "Not that," said Cú Chulainn. "What's that mountain over there?"

' "Sliab Monduirn, Fist Mountain," said the charioteer.

' "Let's go there," said Cú Chulainn.

'So they went there, and when they had reached the mountain, Cú Chulainn said:

' "What's that white cairn yonder on the mountain top?"

' "Finncarn, the White Cairn," said the charioteer.

' "What plain is that down there?"

' "Mag mBreg, Bregia Plain," said the charioteer.

'Likewise he told him the name of every fort between Tara and Cennannas. He told him the name of every field and ford, the famous places and their fortresses and hill-forts. Lastly he pointed out the stronghold of the three sons of Nechta Scéne, who were called Fóill (Sleekit), Fannall (Swallow), and Túachell (Shifty).

' "Are they the ones," said Cú Chulainn, "who say the Ulstermen they've killed outnumber those who are alive?"

' "The very same," said the charioteer.

' "Let's meet them," said Cú Chulainn.

' "That would be dangerous," said the charioteer.

' "We're not here to run from danger," said Cú Chulainn.

'So they drove on. They unhitched the horses where the bog and river met, upstream and south from the enemy stronghold. He took the spancel-hoop that was on the standing stone there and threw it as far as his arm was able into the river to let it drift downstream, thus challenging the mark set by the sons of Nechta Scéne. The sons took note of this and set off to find him.

'After throwing the hoop into the river, Cú Chulainn lay down to sleep beside the standing stone, saying to his charioteer:

' "Don't wake me for one or two, but wake me if they all come."

'The charioteer was terrified. He hitched up the horses and got the chariot ready. He pulled at the rugs that were under Cú Chulainn and the furs that were on top of him, trying not to wake him, for Cú Chulainn had told him not to wake him if only one or two came.

'Then all the sons of Nechta Scéne arrived.

' "What have we here?" said one of them.

' "Only a little boy out on his first drive in a chariot," said the charioteer.

' "Then he's one unlucky mother's son," said the warrior. "His first day under arms will be a bad day. Take yourself off our land, and graze your horses here no more."

' "The reins are in my hand," said the charioteer. "We don't want to cause trouble. Can't you see the boy's asleep?"

' "Boy indeed!" said Cú Chulainn, "well, this boy seeks battle with a man."

' "My pleasure," said the warrior.

' "You can have your pleasure in yonder ford," said Cú Chulainn.

' "You'd be well advised," said the charioteer, "to watch this man you're going to fight. His name is Fóill, Sleekit, and if you don't get him at the first go, you won't get him all day."

' "I swear by the god of Ulster that he won't use his sleekit skills against Ulstermen again, once the broad spear of my comrade Conchobar leaves my hand to seek him out. It'll find him like an outlaw's hand!"

'He fired the spear clean through him and it broke his back. He took his weapons and his head for trophies.

'"Watch out for the next man," said the charioteer. "His name is Fannall, Swallow, and he skims the water lightly as a swan or swallow."

'"He won't use his skimming skills against Ulstermen again," said Cú Chulainn. "You've seen how good I am in the pool at Emain."

'They met in the ford. Cú Chulainn killed him, and took his weapons and his head for trophies.

'"Watch out for the next man you have to face," said the charioteer. "His name is Túachell, Shifty, and he's well named, for no weapon has ever got near him."

'"I'm ready for him with my Riddling-Rod,[16] the wily weapon that will make a bloody sieve of him," said Cú Chulainn.

'He fired the spear at him and it tore him to pieces where he stood. Cú Chulainn went up and cut off his head. He gave the head and the weapons to the charioteer.

'Then he heard the cry of their mother, Nechta Scéne. He put the sons' weapons and their heads into the chariot, and said:

'"I won't let go these trophies until we reach Emain Macha."

'They left with the spoils. Then Cú Chulainn said to the charioteer:

'"You promised us good driving. We'll need it now, for after such a great fight, there's sure to be a great chase."

'They drove on to Sliab Fúait. With Cú Chulainn urging the charioteer on, so fast did they drive across Bregia Plain that the horses overtook the wind and the birds in flight, and Cú Chulainn could catch the stone he'd fired from his sling before it hit the ground.

'They reached Sliab Fúait and found a herd of deer before them.

'"What are those frisky animals over there?" said Cú Chulainn.

'"Wild deer," said the charioteer.

'"What would the men of Ulster rather I brought home, a live one or a dead one?"

'"Live would be wonderful," said the charioteer, "for there's not many that could do it. But there's not a man in Ulster hasn't brought back a dead one. You can't take them alive."

'"I can," said Cú Chulainn. "Don't spare the horses, and drive on through the bog."

'The charioteer did so and the horses got bogged down. Cú Chulainn got out of the chariot and grabbed the deer nearest him, the pride of the herd. He brought the deer under control and lashed the horses on through the bog. Then he hitched the deer to the two back shafts of the chariot.

'The next thing they saw before them was a flock of swans.

'"What would the men of Ulster rather I brought in, a live one or a dead one?"

'"The experts take them alive," said the charioteer.

'Cú Chulainn fired a little stone at the birds and brought down eight of them. Then he fired a bigger stone and got twelve more. He did this with his "ricochet-stun-shot".

'"Go you out and get the birds," said Cú Chulainn. "If I go out to get them, this wild stag here will go for you."

'"It's no easy thing for me for me to get out," said the charioteer. "The horses are so fired up I can't get past them, and the iron rims of the chariot-wheels are too sharp for me to get over them, and I can't get past the stag because his antlers stretch from one shaft of the chariot to the other."

'"Step out on to his antlers then," said Cú Chulainn. "I swear by the god of Ulster, I'll threaten him with such a head-butt, and fix my eye on him with such a look, that he'll not even dare to nod his head at you."

'So it was done. Cú Chulainn tied the reins and the chariot-eer stepped out to gather up the birds. Cú Chulainn hitched the birds to the ropes and straps of the chariot. This was how he proceeded to Emain Macha: a wild stag hitched behind, a flock of swans flapping above, and three severed heads in his chariot.

'They reached Emain.

'"There's a man approaching us in a chariot," cried the look-out in Emain Macha. "He's got the bloody heads of his enemies in his chariot, and a flock of wild birds overhead, and a wild stag hitched behind. He'll spill the blood of every soldier in the fort unless you act quickly and send the naked women out to meet him."

'Cú Chulainn turned the left board of his chariot towards Emain to show his disrespect, and he said:

'"I swear by the god of Ulster, that unless a man is sent to fight me, I'll spill the blood of everybody in the fort."

'"Bring on the naked women!" said Conchobar.

'The women of Emain came out to meet him, led by Mugain, the wife of Conchobar Mac Nessa, and they bared their breasts at him.

'"These are the warriors you must take on today," said Mugain.

'He hid his face. The warriors of Emain grabbed him and threw him into a barrel of cold water. The barrel burst to bits about him. They threw him into another barrel and the water boiled up till it seemed it was boiling with fists. By the time they'd put him into a third barrel, he'd cooled down enough just to warm the water through. Then he got out and Mugain the queen wrapped him in a blue cloak with a silver brooch in it, and a hooded tunic. She brought him to sit on Concho-bar's knee, and that was where he sat from then on.

'"Is it any wonder," said Fiacha Mac Fir Febe, "that some-one who did all this when he was seven should triumph against all odds and beat all comers in fair fight, now that he's reached seventeen?"'

# V
# GUERRILLA
# TACTICS

'ADVANCE,' said Ailill.

The army advanced to Mag Mucceda, the Pigkeepers' Plain. Cú Chulainn felled an oak tree in their path, and cut an ogam message on its side. These were the words he wrote:

'No one passes unless a warrior can jump this in a chariot.'

They pitched their tents on the spot and began trying to jump the tree in their chariots. Thirty horses fell and thirty chariots were broken there. Belach nÁne – Jump Pass – is the name of that place ever since.

They stayed there until morning. Fráech Mac Fidach was summoned.

'Help us, Fráech,' said Medb. 'Get us out of this fix. See if you can find Cú Chulainn and get him to fight.'

Early next morning Fráech set out with a squad of nine and came to Áth Fúait. He saw the hero bathing in the river.

'Wait here,' said Fráech to the squad, 'and I'll tackle him where he is. He's not good in water.'

He stripped off and approached him in the water.

'Come any closer,' said Cú Chulainn, 'and you die. I'd be sorry to kill you.'

'I'm coming,' said Fráech, 'to meet you in the water. Rules of fair fight.'

'Choose your style of combat,' said Cú Chulainn.

'The one-arm grapple,' said Fráech.

They grappled for a long time in the water, and Fráech went under. Cú Chulainn dragged him up.

'Now,' said Cú Chulainn, 'will you give in, so I can spare your life?'

'Not me,' said Fráech.

Cú Chulainn held him under until Fráech died. He was brought to land. They carried his body to the camp. Ever since, that ford has been called Áth Fraích.

The whole camp mourned Fráech. They saw a company of women dressed in green gowns appear around the body of Fráech Mac Fidach. They bore him into the fairy mound. Ever since, it has been called Síd[1] Fraích, Fráech's Fairy Mound.

Then Fergus jumped the oak tree in his chariot.

They went on till they came to Áth Táiten, Kidnappers' Ford. Cú Chulainn finished six of the army off, the six Dúngals of Irros.

They went on again and came to Fornocht, the Bare Place. Medb had a puppy dog called Baiscne – Timber. Cú Chulainn slung a stone at it and took off its head. Ever since, the place has been called Druim Baiscne, Timber Ridge.

'Every one of you will be a laughing-stock,' said Medb, 'unless you hunt down this mad animal that's been picking you off.'

So they set off; and they hunted him till the shafts of their chariots broke.

The next morning they went to Iraird Cuillenn. Cú Chulainn went on ahead of them. At the place called Tamlachta Órláim, Órlám's Burial Mound, just north of the sanctuary Dísert Lochait, he came across Órlám's charioteer. Órlám – Golden-arm – was a son of Ailill and Medb. Cú Chulainn took the charioteer for an Ulsterman.

'If there are Ulstermen out here,' he said, 'they're out on a limb, for the army is on their track.'

He went up warn the charioteer, and saw he was cutting wood for a chariot-shaft.

'What are you up to?' said Cú Chulainn.

'Cutting holly shafts for a chariot,' said the charioteer. 'We broke our chariots hunting that wild animal Cú Chulainn. Give us a hand – do you want to cut the shafts, or trim them?'

'I'll trim,' said Cú Chulainn.

The charioteer watched as Cú Chulainn stripped the shafts from bark to knot with sweeps of his outstretched fingers. When they left his hand they were so slippery-clean a fly couldn't have settled on them.

'I put you to the wrong class of work,' said the charioteer. He was very afraid.

'Who owns you?' said Cúchulain.

'I'm Órlám's charioteer. That's *the* Órlám, son of Ailill and Medb. And you?' said the charioteer.

'My name is Cú Chulainn.'

'Then I'm done for,' said the charioteer.

'There's nothing to fear,' said Cú Chulainn. 'Where's your master?'

'Over there, by the ditch,' said the charioteer.

'Then come with me now,' said Cú Chulainn, 'for I don't kill charioteers.'

Cú Chulainn went up to Órlám. He killed him and cut off his head, and waved the head at the army. He set the head on the charioteer's back and said:

'Take this back to the camp with you. If you don't do as I say, there'll be a stone from my sling for you.'

When the charioteer got near the camp, he took the head from his back and told Ailill and Medb of his adventure.

'It's not like catching wee birds,' she said.

'And he said if I didn't bring the head to the camp on my back, he'd break my head for me with a stone.'

The three sons of Gárach were waiting at their ford. Their names: Lon, Úalu and Díliu – Blackbird, Proud and Flood. Their charioteers, the three foster-sons Mes Lir, Mes Lóech and Mes Lethan. They thought Cú Chulainn had overstepped the mark in killing the king's two foster-sons, besides killing his son and waving the head at the army. They made a plan to kill Cú Chulainn and so snuff out the threat to their forces. They cut three wooden cudgels for their charioteers so that all six could gang up on him. He killed the lot, for they'd broken the rules of fair fight.

Órlám's charioteer was standing between Ailill and Medb. Cú Chulainn slung a stone at him and opened his head for him so that his brain came out around his ears. His name was Fertedil, the Entitled Man. It wasn't true that Cú Chulainn didn't kill charioteers. He killed them when they deserved it.

Cú Chulainn issued a threat in Méithe that any time he got sight of Ailill or Medb, he would fire a stone from his sling at them. So he did: he slung a stone and killed a pet stoat as it sat on Medb's shoulder by her neck, south of the ford. Hence the name Méithe Togmaill, Stoat Neck. North of the ford he killed the pet bird perched on Ailill's shoulder. Hence Méithe nEoin, Bird Neck. And at this time also, Reúin was drowned in the lake which bears his name.

'The man you're up against is not far off,' said Ailill to his sons, the Maines.

They rose to their feet and looked around. They were settling down again when Cú Chulainn struck. He slung a stone at one of them and broke his head.

'That was some uprising,' said Maenén[2] the jester, 'after all your big talk. Me, I would have taken his head off.'

Cú Chulainn slung a stone at him and broke his head.

This, then, is how they became casualties: firstly, Órlám on the mound called after him; the three sons of Gárach at the ford called after them; Fertedil between royalty; and Maenén on the mound called after him.

'I swear by the god my people swear by,' said Ailill, 'that I'll cut in two any man who mocks Cú Chulainn from now on. Let's proceed to Cúailnge, travelling by day and night. If things go on like this, that man will kill two thirds of our army.'

Then the harpers of the Venerable Tree of Caín Bile came
from the Red Cataract of Ess Ruad to play for them. The
Connachtmen took them for spies sent by Ulster. They hunted
them until they turned into deer and vanished into the
standing-stones at Lía Mór, for they were druids of great
power.

Lethan – the Broad – came to his ford on the river Níth in
Conaille. Galled by Cú Chulainn's deeds, he lay in wait for
him. Cú Chulainn cut off his head and left it with the body.
Hence the name Áth Lethan, Broad Ford. Many chariots
were broken in the fighting just before that in the next ford.
Hence the name Áth Carpat, Chariot Ford. Lethan's charioteer, Mulcha – the Boss – was cut down on the shoulder-ridge
that lies between the two fords. Hence Guala Mulchaí, Boss
Shoulder.

The next day the Irish army began to lay waste Bregia Plain
and Muirthemne Plain. Fergus felt it in his bones that his
foster-son Cú Chulainn was nearby, and told the men to be
on their guard against him. For he knew that though they
would not find Cú Chulainn, he would find them. As the army
crossed the plain, the Morrígan – the Nightmare Queen[3] –
came in the form of a bird and settled on a standing-stone in
Temair Cúailnge, and chanted these words to the Brown Bull:

restless does the Dark Bull     know death-dealing slaughter
secret that the raven     wrings from writhing soldiers
as the Dark One grazes     on the dark green grasses
waving meadows blossoming     with necks and flowers
lowing cattle of the Badb     the groans of battle
armies ground to dust     the raven struts on corpses
war-clouds raging over     Cúailnge day and night
kith and kin lie down     to join the tribes of dead

Then the Bull made his way to Sliab Culinn with his entourage of fifty heifers, followed by his keeper, who was called
Forgaimen – the Skin Rug.[4] The Bull threw off the three fifties

of young fellows that used to play on his back and killed two thirds of them. In Cúailnge he dug a trench through Tír Marccéni – the Land of the Plumed Horses – before he went, throwing the earth up after him with his heels.

Here are some of the qualities of the Donn Cúailnge:

He could bull fifty heifers every day. They'd calve at the same hour the next day, and those that didn't would burst, overwhelmed as they were by the offspring of the Brown Bull. Fifty grown young fellows would play games every evening on the broad of his back. His shadow could shelter a hundred warriors from heat or cold. Another of his qualities was this, that no ghost or gremlin or battle-demon would dare approach the zone in which he stood. And every evening as he came to his byre the bass swell of his lowing resounded throughout the four quarters of Cúailnge to make great music for its people.

The next day the army advanced through the rocks and dunes of Conaille Muirthemne. Medb ordered a tortoise-shell of shields to be placed over her in case Cú Chulainn should fire a stone at her from the hills or the heights. But he made no attack that day.

Cú Chulainn was at Sliab Cuincu, Yoke Mountain, when the army arrived in Cúailnge and pitched their tents. Medb told one of her handmaids, Lóchu, to go and fetch her water from the river. So Lóchu went with an escort of fifty women. Cú Chulainn took her for Medb. He slung a stone at her from the heights of Cuincu and killed her on the flat place that bears her name, Réid Lócha, Lócha's Level, in Cúailnge.

From Finnabair Cúailnge the army fanned out and set fire to the district. They rounded up the women, boys, girls and cattle and brought them to Finnabair.

'Not such a good take,' said Medb. 'I see you haven't got the bull.'

'He's nowhere to be found in the province,' said everyone.

Lóthar – the Tub – one of Medb's cattlemen, was summoned.

'Where, in your humble opinion,' said she, 'is the bull?'

'I tremble to tell you,' said the Tub, 'but the night the Ulstermen were laid low by the Curse, he took off with sixty heifers, and he's now at the Black Whirlpool of Dubchoire in Glenn Gatt.'

'Go,' said Medb. 'Each pair of men, take an osier shackle.'

So they did. Hence the name Glenn Gatt, Osier Glen.

Then they brought the bull to Finnabair. When the bull caught sight of the Tub, he went for him and ripped out his guts with his horns. He ran amok through the camp with his entourage of three fifties of heifers, and fifty warriors were killed.

Then the bull vanished and they were at their wits' end as to where.

Medb asked another of her cattlemen where he thought the bull might be.

'I think he might be in the innermost recesses of Sliab Culinn.'

They went there, laying waste to Cúailnge on the way, but found no bull. The river Cronn rose up against them as high as the tree-tops so that they spent the night by the water's edge. Medb ordered a select few of her people to cross the Cronn.

The next morning a hero attempted it. His name was Úalu. He shouldered a great flagstone to steady him against the current. The river upended him, stone and all. His grave and stone are still there on the roadside by the river. They call it Lia Úalann, Úalu's Standing Stone.

It was there that Cú Chulainn killed Cronn and Cóemdele in a furious attack. A hundred warriors died at his hand, among them Róan and Roae, two chroniclers of the Táin. A gross of kings were killed by him beside the same river.

Then the army skirted the river Cronn as far as its source, and would have crossed the mountain between source and summit, but Medb had other ideas. She preferred to cross the mountain by leaving a track that would show forever her contempt for Ulster. It took them three days and three nights

to dig up the terrain before them to make the Pass of the
Cúailnge Cattle, Bernas Bó Cúailnge.

Then they went through the Pass of the Cúailnge Cattle
with all the cattle of Cúailnge. They spent the night at Glenn
Dáil Imda, the Glen of the Great Gathering, in Cúailnge. That
place is also called Botha on account of the bothies they built
there. The next day they went on to the river Colptha – the
river of the Yearling Heifers. Recklessly they attempted a
crossing. It rose up against them and swept a hundred charioteers into the sea. That place is now called Cluain Carpat,
Chariot Water-Meadow. They skirted the Colptha up to its
source at Bélat Ailóin and spent the night at Liasa Liac, the
Flagstone Sheds, so called because of the stone shelters they
built there for their calves. They came through Glenn Gatlaig
and the river Gatlaig rose up against them. Previously it had
been called the Sechaire, Meander, but from then on it was
called the Gatlaig, Osier, because they'd taken the calves over
tied with osiers. They spent the night in Druim Féne, Warrior
Ridge, in Conaille.

That was how they fared from Cúailnge to the plain of
Machaire according to this version. But other authorities
and other books give a different account of events as they
proceeded from Finnabair to Conaille, as follows:

When they had assembled with their plunder in Finnabair in
Cúailnge, Medb said:

'Split up the army. We're too many to go by the one road.
Let Ailill take half by way of Mídluachair. We'll go with
Fergus through the Ulster Pass, Bernas Bó nUlad.'

'The half we're left with,' said Fergus, 'is not the better half.
We'll have to cut through the mountain to make a road for
the cattle.'

So they did, whence the name Bernas Bó nUlad, Ulster
Cattle Pass.

Then Ailill said to his charioteer Cuillius:[5]

'Spy on Medb and Fergus for me today. I don't know why

they're keeping such close company, and it would please me if you brought me a clue.'

Cuillius came across the pair of them in Cluichre, the Shelter. They had dallied there while the army went on ahead. They did not hear Cuillius as he came into their presence. It so happened that Fergus's sword was lying beside him. Cuillius drew it from its sheath and left the sheath empty. Cuillius went to Ailill.

'So?' said Ailill.

'So indeed,' said Cuillius. 'Here's your clue.'

'So far so good,' said Ailill.

They smiled at one another.

'Just as you thought,' said Cuillius, 'I found them in bed together.'

'It's right for her,' said Ailill. 'She did it to help the campaign. Keep the sword in good order. Wrap it in linen and put it under the seat of your chariot.'

Fergus looked round for his sword.

'I am undone,' he said.

'What's the matter?' said Medb.

'The bad turn I've done Ailill,' he said. 'Wait here till I come back from the wood,' said Fergus, 'and don't wonder if I'm gone for some time.'

Medb didn't know that the sword had gone. He went away from her, carrying the sword of his charioteer. He hewed a sword from a tree in the wood. Hence the Ulster name for it, Fid Mórthruaille, Big Scabbard Wood.

'Let's catch up with the others,' said Fergus.

The two halves of the army met on the plain. They pitched their tents. Ailill sent for Fergus to play chess.[6] When Fergus came into the tent Ailill began laughing at him. Fergus said:

> better the man    who is mocked    if not deluded
> by his damned deed    sword-tip seared    by Macha's
>                                           scorn
>    Gailéoin blades    grim outcry    vengeance thwarted

by a woman's will    likewise lying    bloody corpses
captured    herds    spears
crushed against    Cú Chulainn's mountain    likewise
trunkless heads    tumbled    struggle

Ailill said:

declare no war    your weapon lost    in the deep ford
of a royal belly    pastures sicken    standing stones cry
                                              out
dark father    Medb    among seething tribes
backbiting witnesses    of the wild wood    struggling with
rambling women    however they come    arms clamouring
through the fog likewise    of tumultuous deeds

'Sit yourself down,' said Ailill. 'Let's play chess. You're
welcome here.' And Ailill said:

play chess    and draughts[7]    face to face
with king and queen    the field prepared    and eager
for armies    in iron companies    no matter for what
stakes you play    I know    the game well
likewise queens and women    true what they say
the first fault theirs    their sweet companionable wrath
Finnabair's dear shield    valorous Fergus
with bellowing herds    at the heart    of his forces
in regal form    with dragon-blaze    and viper-hiss
and lion-slash    forever to the fore    Fergus Mac Rossa
                                              Róich

They began to play chess. They moved the gold and silver
men across the bronze board. And Ailill said:

it's not right for a king    so sweet and slender
to be borne by death    on a bronze point    more beautiful
the frenzied board    imperious Medb    brought down

these wise men    I move against Fergus
likewise    as we play out    the vengeful game

Medb said:

leave off these words    so wild and foolish
unfit for a queen    the furtive love
of glib strangers    a judgement that is not
unjust    no havoc wrought    shun
the cattlemen    likewise    caterwauling
    Fergus in the clear

Fergus was heard to say:

alas    they spout words    hawkish
to this tribe    and that likewise    fed by backbiters
by secret gold    bewitched    by javelins
wiped out    likewise royalty    brought down
    mocked    at your command

They stayed there that night. Next morning Ailill was heard
to say:

one great soldier    faces the huge forces
by Cronn's dark water    O'Nessa's stream
his deeds fulfilled    in Connacht combat
blood streams    from headless necks    likewise
where heroes congregate    a parliament of graves
floodwaters rise    against the beardless one
    the Ulster champion

Medb spoke:

keep sword in sheath    O arrogant Mac Máta
while chariots tumble    from stony heights
men herded    women snatched

likewise cattle    and a multitude    of heads
swords broken    on all sides    heroic deeds
wrought in murk    oxen driven    women
likewise    great armies    turning from
the battle plain of Cúailnge    O sleeping army

Fergus was heard:

a great head spiked    on the scythed hub
of a chariot wheel    the features    bold as brass
let them swear    likewise    by their people
render    oaths unto their queen    bear arms
    against whatever    enemy

Medb was heard:

let it be done    according to his word
let it be done    for he is yoked    as to a breast
to your command    the armies march
while Ailill's power    is in your hands
    against whatever    enemy

They advanced to the river Cronn. Maine, a son of Aillil,
was heard to say:

send me    on an urgent mission
to take on    the blond forceful man
who keeps off    father and mother
from the horned cattle    likewise to leap
into a chariot    with forceful feat
to wipe clean    the battle field

Fergus was heard:

don't go son    brave and all    as you are
they'll only say    your head    will be cut

from its neck     by the beardless boy     who hurls
insults     from the heights     to the plains
summons up     rivers     shakes     the woods
wrenches     into shape     great deeds
a power of water     crowds     of drowned
Ailill laid low     Medb mocked     faces turned
　　　by sword and spear

'Let me go ahead with the exiles,' said Fergus, 'to see that
the lad gets fair play, with the cattle out front, the army in
back, and the women following.'
　Medb was heard:

listen Fergus     for the sake of     your good name
guard these cattle     with your     good army
subjugate     with rage     the Ulstermen
are not     easily cast down     on the plain of Aí
assemble     where     the tracks confer

Fergus said:

for pity's sake Medb     listening     I'm not
before the tribe     your pliable boy
to struggle through     the battle-mist     in Emain
no more     to rain blows     on the tribe
cast no stone     at the back of my neck
what good is that     at the heels of the hunt

Cú Chulainn came to meet them at the ford on the Cronn.
　'Comrade Láeg,' he said to his charioteer, 'the army is
closing in.'
　Láeg said:

I swear by the gods     I'll do great deeds
among charioteers     driving through     the battle-zone
borne     by slender steeds     with silver yokes

> and golden wheels    to roll over    royal heads
> leaping onwards    to victory

Cú Chulainn said:

> now Láeg    grasp the reins
> tear through    the fray    for Macha's victory
> like women    running    after sons
> through pinewoods    over    crackling pine-cones
> erupt against    Ailill and Medb    impress
> triumphant    stamp    upon their face

'I summon the waters to come to my aid,' said Cú Chulainn.
'I summon heaven and earth and above all the Cronn.'

> The black waters of the Cronn
> will keep them from Muirthemne,
> until soldier's work be done
> up North at Mount Ocháine.

And the water rose to the tree-tops.

Maine, a son of Ailill and Medb, came forward before the
rest. Cú Chulainn put an end to him in the ford, and thirty
horsemen of his household were drowned. A further thirty-
two soldiers were killed by him in the ford.

They pitched their tents by the same ford. Lugaid Mac
Nóis Uí Lomairc Allchomaig went out with a troop of thirty
horse-soldiers to parley with Cú Chulainn.

'Well met, Lugaid,' said Cú Chulainn. 'If a flock of wildfowl
settled on Muirthemne Plain, I'd give you a goose and share
another; if fish crowded the river-mouths, I'd give you a salmon and share another, and I'd give you three sprigs of herb
besides – watercress, brooklime and sea samphire. And a man
to stand for you at the ford of battle.'

'I believe it,' said Lugaid. 'I wish a wealth of followers for the same lad.'

'Fine army you have there,' said Cú Chulainn.

'Well, there's more of them than there are of you. But that'll not daunt you.'

'All I need is fair play and fair fight,' said Cú Chulainn. 'Comrade Lugaid,' he said, 'is your army afraid of me?'

'I swear to god,' said Lugaid, 'that not one or two of them dares to piss outside the camp, but twenty or thirty of them have to go.'

'Maybe they'd go somewhere else,' said Cú Chulainn, 'if I began pelting them with my sling. And should they come to pit their strength against mine, you'd do well to remember your closeness to the men of Ulster. Now tell me, Lugaid, what it is you want.'

'I want a ceasefire for my men.'

'You have it, so long as they wear a badge. And tell my comrade Fergus that his men must wear a badge too. Tell the doctors to wear badges, and to swear to look after my life, and to bring me food every night.'

Lugaid left him. It happened that Fergus was in Ailill's tent. Lugaid called him out and delivered the message.

Ailill was heard to say:

> proper is it    this whispering advice
> the pleasant plain    the poisoned fort    well supplied
> for our great army    he picks off    our people
> for the sake of    Róech's son    so we hear
> assisted as we are    by Medb's sweet foray
> why not take    a select band    to a special tent
> protected against    this onslaught    of stones and sods
> a secret gathering    if he come near

'I swear to god it can't be done,' said Fergus, 'without going to the lad again. Do this, Lugaid. Ask him if he'll let Ailill and his division of three thousand join mine. And bring him an ox and a salt pig and a hogshead of wine.'

Lugaid went and asked.

'It's no odds to me,' said Cú Chulainn, 'what he does.'

So the two divisions combined. They stayed there for the night – or twenty nights, as some versions have it. Cú Chulainn picked off thirty soldiers with his sling.

'Things are not getting any better,' said Fergus. 'The Ulstermen will soon be over the Curse, and then they'll grind us into dirt and dust. We're not well placed to do battle. Let's advance to Cúil Airthir.'

Meanwhile Cú Chulainn reported back to the Ulstermen.

'What news?' said Conchobar.

'Women raped, cattle plundered, men murdered,' said Cú Chulainn.

'Who rapes? Who plunders? Who murders?' said Conchobar.

Cú Chulainn said:

> foremost in rape     plunder and pillage
> Aillil Mac Máta     Fergus Mac Róich
> superlative swordsman     wolf-like in battle
> the key     to Conchobar's lock

'We're not much use,' said Conchobar. 'We got the Curse again today.'

As Cú Chulainn was leaving he saw the army advance. Ailill said:

> O grief     I see     a chariot
> glittering     with spear-points     soldiers
> going under     dark water     herds
> driven     blood pouring     from headless
> necks     men for     Ulster cattle     fighting
> falling     by the crux     of the ford

Cú Chulainn killed thirty soldiers at Áth Durn, the Ford of the Fist. The army made a forced march to Cúil Airthir. It was dusk when they arrived. He killed another thirty there before they had pitched their tents.

The next morning Ailill's charioteer Cuillius was at the ford washing the wheels of his chariot. Cú Chulainn slung a stone at him and killed him. Hence the name Áth Cuillne, the Ford of Cuillius, at Cúil Airthir.

They travelled on and spent the night at Druim Féine in Conaille – and that is how they reached that place, according to the second version.

Cú Chulainn kept sniping at them. For each of the three nights they were encamped there he killed a hundred men, picking them off with his sling from the nearby heights of Ocháine.

# VI
# SINGLE
# COMBAT

'AT THIS RATE,' said Ailill, 'our army won't last long. Make him an offer – he can have a piece of the Plain of Aí as big as Muirthemne Plain itself, plus the best chariot in Aí, plus equipment for a dozen soldiers. Or, if he prefers, the plain where he was brought up, plus twenty-one bond-maids, plus compensation for whatever of his we might have destroyed, whether cattle or household goods. And let him serve under me. He'd be better off with me than with that excuse for a lord he serves now.'

'Who'll deliver the message?'

'Mac Roth yonder.'

Mac Roth, the messenger of Ailill and Medb – Mac Roth who could make a circuit of all Ireland in one day – went to Delga, the Spike, with the message. It was Fergus's understanding that Cú Chulainn was in Delga.

There had been a big snow that night and all of Ireland was one white plain.

'I see a man approach,' said Láeg to Cú Chulainn. 'He has yellow hair. He carries a linen ensign. A great truncheon in his hand. An ivory-hilted sword at his waist. He wears a red-embroidered hooded tunic.'

'That'll be a messenger sent to parley with me,' said Cú Chulainn.

Mac Roth asked Láeg whom he served under.

'I serve under that man over there,' said Láeg.

Cú Chulainn was sitting thigh-deep in the snow, without a

stitch on, picking lice from his shirt. Mac Roth asked whom he served under.

'I serve under Conchobar Mac Nessa,' said Cú Chulainn.

'Could you give more detail?'

'I gave detail enough,' said Cú Chulainn.

'Then can you tell me where Cú Chulainn is?' said Mac Roth.

'What would you have to say to him?' said Cú Chulainn.

Mac Roth gave him Ailill's message.

'If Cú Chulainn were here he wouldn't agree to that. He wouldn't swap his mother's brother for another king.'

Mac Roth went back to Ailill and Medb.

'Did you not find him?' said Medb.

'I found a surly fierce angry fellow in Delga. Whether he is the notorious Cú Chulainn, I couldn't say.'

'Did he accept the offer?'

'Indeed he did not,' said Mac Roth, and he told them why not.

'It was Cú Chulainn that you spoke to,' said Fergus.

'Offer him other terms,' said Medb.

'Such as?' said Ailill.

'The freewomen and the dry cows from our plunder, so long as he doesn't attack us with his sling by night, no matter about the day,' said Medb.

'Who'll go?' said Ailill.

'Who but Mac Roth?' said Medb.

'I'll go,' said Mac Roth, 'now I know the lie of the land.'

Mac Roth went back to Cú Chulainn and delivered the message.

'I can't agree to that,' said Cú Chulainn, 'for if they keep the bondwomen, the freewomen will have to work at grinding grain, and if they keep the milch cows, we'll have no milk.'

Mac Roth went back to Cú Chulainn again and said he could have the bondwomen and the milch cows instead.

'I can't agree to that,' said Cú Chulainn, 'for the men of Ulster would lie with the bondwomen and breed low-class bastards, and they'd kill the milch cows for meat in the winter.'

'Are there any terms that would do you?' said the messenger.

'There are,' said Cú Chulainn, 'but I'm not telling you. If you can find someone who knows what they are, it's a deal.'

'I know what he means,' said Fergus. 'Not that it's much good to you. These are his terms: the cattle to stay by the ford, while he engages the army in single combat on a daily basis. He's playing for time until help arrives from the Ulstermen. Mind you, I'm surprised they're taking so long to get over the Curse.'

'Better for us,' said Ailill, 'to lose one man every day than a hundred every night.'

Fergus went to Cú Chulainn with those terms. He was followed by Etarcomol,[1] a foster-son of Ailill and Medb, and son of Ed and Leithrenn.[2]

'I'd prefer it if you didn't come,' said Fergus. 'Not that I don't like you, but I don't relish the thought of a fight between you and Cú Chulainn. What with your insolence and pride, and his mad ferocity and violent fury, it would not be a good meeting.'

'Can I not be under your protection?' said Etarcomol.

'You can,' said Fergus, 'so long as you don't disrespect him if he speaks to you.'

They took two chariots to Delga.

It happened that Cú Chulainn was playing draughts with Láeg. Cú Chulainn had his back to the chariots and Láeg was facing towards them.

'I see two chariots approaching,' said Láeg. 'In the leading chariot is a tall swarthy man with a full head of dark hair. He wears a purple cloak with a gold brooch, and a red-embroidered hooded tunic. He carries a curved shield with a scalloped trim of white gold, and a broad spear with an ornamented shaft. At his hip is a sword as big as the rudder of a boat.'

'A great big useless rudder,' said Cú Chulainn, 'for that's my comrade Fergus. He carries no sword in his scabbard but a wooden sword. As I heard it, Ailill caught him off guard as he slept with Medb, and made off with Fergus's sword, and gave it to his charioteer for safe keeping. A wooden sword was put in the scabbard.'

At that point Fergus arrived.

'Well met, comrade Fergus,' said Cú Chulainn. 'If fishes crowded the river-mouths, I'd give you a salmon and share another; if a flock of wildfowl landed on the plain, I'd give you a goose and share another, with a fistful of watercress or marshwort or samphire and a drink from the sand. And there'd be a man to stand for you against all comers at the ford, to watch for you while you slept.'

'I believe it,' said Fergus, 'but it wasn't for the food that I came. I know what you have in store.'

Fergus offered Cúchulainn the terms, and left.

Etarcomol stayed behind, staring at Cú Chulainn.

'What are you looking at?' said Cú Chulainn.

'You,' said Etarcomol.

'An eye could soon take that in,' said Cú Chulainn.

'So I see,' said Etarcomol. 'I find nothing to be afraid of. No horror or terror, nothing that could take on an army. You're just a pretty boy with fancy skills and toy weapons.'

'You disrespect me,' said Cú Chulainn, 'but for Fergus's sake I won't kill you. If it weren't for his protection, your guts would be strung out behind you and your quarters scattered all the way from your chariot to the camp.'

'You needn't try to threaten me,' said Etarcomol. 'As for your wonderful deal, to engage in single combat, I'll be the first one of the men of Ireland to fight you tomorrow.'

He went off. Between Méithe and Ceithe he turned back, saying to his charioteer:

'I swore in front of Fergus,' he said, 'that I'd fight Cú Chulainn tomorrow. But I can't wait till then. Turn the horses at this hill.'

Láeg saw this and said to Cú Chulainn:

'The chariot's coming back. He's turned his left board against us.'

'Such a challenge can't be refused,' said Cú Chulainn. 'Drive down to the ford to meet him, and we'll see what comes of it.'

'I don't want this,' said Cú Chulainn, 'though you've asked for it.'

'But you must do it,' said Etarcomol.

Cú Chulainn cut the sod from under his feet and he fell over with the sod on his belly.

'Take yourself off,' said Cú Chulainn. 'I don't relish the thought of having to wash my hands after you. But for Fergus, I'd have cut you to pieces long ago.'

'We can't part like this,' said Etarcomol. 'Either I take your head, or leave you mine.'

'The latter for sure,' said Cú Chulainn.

He waved his sword at Etarcomol's two armpits and the clothes fell off him, leaving his skin unscathed.

'Now will you go away?' said Cú Chulainn.

'On the contrary,' said Etarcomol.

Cú Chulainn waved his sword over him and cut off his hair that close to his head you'd think it was done with a razor. There wasn't so much as a scratch on his scalp. But the fellow persisted in his contrariness and Cú Chulainn brought his sword down through the crown of his head and split him to the navel.

Fergus saw the chariot passing him with only one man in it, and he went back to give off to Cú Chulainn.

'You twisted little devil,' he said, 'you've let me down badly. You must think I've a very short prick.'

'Don't be angry with me, comrade Fergus,' said Cú Chulainn,

woman's pride    provoking rivalry
brought this about    who fled    from Ulster
absent    sword of glory    brought this

> rival edge     down through     Etarcomol's yoke
> of haughty snub     death blossoming     through that
> which was     wrapped up     sheathed beneath
> a chariot seat     neither sleeping     nor eating
> restless     for the steady hand     that held me
> once     do not scold me     comrade Fergus

He fell prostrate and Fergus's chariot went over him three times.

'Ask his charioteer if I was the one who started it.'

'Indeed you were not,' said the charioteer.

'He declared,' said Cú Chulainn, 'that he wouldn't go away without taking my head, or leaving his. Which would you prefer, comrade Fergus?'

'I prefer what was done,' said Fergus, 'for he was too haughty by half.'

Fergus put a spancel-hoop through Etarcomol's heels and dragged him behind his chariot back to the camp. Whenever they went over rocky ground, the two halves of the body came apart; on smooth ground they came together again.

Medb took a look.

'Rough treatment for a young dog,' said Medb.

'He was an ignorant pup,' said Fergus, 'to pick a fight with a great hound.'

A grave was dug for him. A stone was put up for him. His name was written in ogam. An elegy was made for him.

Cú Chulainn attacked no one with his sling that night.

'Who have you got to take on Cú Chulainn tomorrow?' said Lugaid.

'Maybe tomorrow will tell,' said Maine, one of Ailill's sons.

'We've no one to take him on,' said Medb. 'Ask him for a truce while we go and look for someone.'

That was agreed.

'Where should we begin to look,' said Ailill, 'for a man to take on Cú Chulainn?'

'His match,' said Medb, 'is not to be found in Ireland, unless we can get Cú Roí or the warrior Nad Crantail.'[3]

One of Cú Roí's men was in the tent.

'You won't get Cú Roí,' he said. 'He feels he's done enough in getting his men to come here.'

'Then send for Nad Crantail.'

Maine Andoe the Quick Man went to Nad Crantail and told him what they had in mind.

'Come with us for the honour of Connacht.'

'I won't go,' said Nad Crantail, 'unless they give me their daughter Finnabair.'

He came then. They brought his weapons in a cart from East Connacht to the camp.

'You can have Finnabair,' said Medb, 'if you take on that man.'

'Done,' said Nad Crantail.

Lugaid went to Cú Chulainn that night.

'Nad Crantail is coming to take you on tomorrow. It doesn't look good for you. He's unbeatable.'

'No odds to me,' said Cú Chulainn.

Nad Crantail left the camp the next morning and took nine holly stakes with him, sharpened and hardened by fire. He came across Cú Chulainn out wildfowling, with his chariot nearby. Nad Crantail fired a stake at Cú Chulainn. Cú Chulainn made one of his trick jumps on to the point of the stake, never taking his eyes off his prey. Likewise with the other eight stakes. As the ninth stake was fired at him, the flock of birds flew away from Cú Chulainn, and he sped off after them. Like a bird himself he stepped from point to point of the flying stakes in his haste not to let the birds escape. But to everyone it seemed that Cú Chulainn was flying from Nad Crantail.

'That Cú Chulainn of yours,' said Nad Crantail, 'has flown from me.'

'It was only to be expected,' said Medb, 'that if a true warrior came, the little imp would take off.'

Fergus and the Ulstermen were very put out by this. Fiacha Mac Fir Febe was sent to take Cú Chulainn to task.

'Tell him,' said Fergus, 'that it was glorious when he stood against many men in battle. But it would be more glorious for him to hide his face now after fleeing from one man, for he shames the men of Ulster as well as himself.'

'Who's bragging about this?' said Cú Chulainn.

'Nad Crantail,' said Fiacha.

'Had he bragged me up for the trick I performed before his very eyes, it would have been more to the point,' said Cú Chulainn. 'But had he met me with a real weapon in his hand, he wouldn't be bragging now. You know I don't kill unarmed men. Let him come tomorrow between Ocháine and the sea; however early he comes, he'll find me waiting, and I'll not fly from him.'

Cú Chulainn went to the meeting place. After watching all night he threw on his cloak, not noticing that beside him was a standing stone as big as himself, and it went with him under the cloak.

Then Nad Crantail arrived with his cartful of weapons.

'Where's Cú Chulainn?' he said.

'Over there,' said Fergus.

'He's not the same shape as he was yesterday,' said Nad Crantail. 'Are you Cú Chulainn?'

'What if I am?' said Cú Chulainn.

'If you are,' said Nad Crantail, 'then I'd rather take a little lamb's head back to the camp, for yours is the head of a beardless boy.'

'I'm not him either,' said Cú Chulainn. 'You'll find him behind that hill.'

Cú Chulainn went over to Láeg.

'Put a blackberry beard on me. This warrior won't fight unless I have a beard.'

This was done for him. He went to meet Nad Crantail on the hill.

'That's better,' said Nad Crantail. 'Now, let's have a fight with rules.'

'But of course. Whatever you say,' said Cú Chulainn.

'We'll fire spears at each other,' said Nad Crantail, 'but no dodging.'

'No dodging except upwards,' said Cú Chulainn.

Nad Crantail fired his spear at him but Cú Chulainn jumped in the air as it reached him. It struck the standing stone and broke in two.

'Foul! You dodged!' said Nad Crantail.

'You're allowed to dodge upwards too,' said Cú Chulainn.

Cú Chulainn fired his spear, but upwards, so that it landed on the crown of Nad Crantail's head and went through him into the ground.

'Good grief,' he said. 'Truly, you are the best warrior in Ireland. I have twenty-four sons in the camp. Let me go and tell them about my hidden treasure. Then I'll come back and you can cut off my head, for if this spear is taken out I'll die anyway.'

'Fair enough,' said Cú Chulainn. 'But do come back.'

Nad Crantail went to the camp. They all came out to meet him, saying,

'Where is the head of the Torqued Man?'

'Warriors, hold on. I have something to tell my sons. Then I'm going back to deal with Cú Chulainn.'

He went back after Cú Chulainn, and threw his sword at him. Cú Chulainn jumped into the air. He became terribly transformed, as he had with the young fellows in Emain. He landed on Nad Crantail's shield and cut off his head. He struck again through the headless neck and split him to the navel. The four bits fell to the ground.

Then Cú Chulainn chanted this verse:

> Now that Nad Crantail is dead
> the fight goes on but more so.
> Right now I could ply my blade
> on a third of Medb's army.

# VII
# THEY FIND
# THE BULL

# MEDB TOOK A THIRD of her army

to Cuib to look for the bull, and Cú Chulainn tailed her. She took the Midluachair Road then, advancing against the Ulster folk and the Cruithin as far north as Dún Sobairche, the Primrose Fort.

Cú Chulainn saw a thing: Buide Mac Báin[1] coming from Sliab Culinn with the bull and fifteen heifers, and an escort of sixty men of Ailill's household, every man of them cloaked. Cú Chulainn went up to them.

'Where did you get the cattle?' said Cú Chulainn.

'From yonder mountain,' said one of the soldiers.

'Where's their herdsman?' said Cú Chulainn.

'Where we found him,' said the soldier.

Cú Chulainn took three bounds over to the ford to talk to their leader.

'What is your name?' he said.

'One who's neither friend nor foe – Buide Mac Báin,' he said.

'Here's a spear for Buide,' said Cú Chulainn.

He drove a javelin into his armpit and the point ended up making two bits of his liver. He died by his ford, called Áth mBuide because of him.

The bull was brought into the camp.

Then it was decided that a Cú Chulainn deprived of his javelin would cause no more trouble than the next man. Redg,[2] Ailill's satirist, was sent to get the javelin from him.

'Give me the javelin,' said the satirist.

'Not that,' said Cú Chulainn, 'but I'll give you something just as dear.'

'I'd rather you didn't,' said the satirist.

Cú Chulainn gave him a slap because he wouldn't accept his offer. Redg threatened him with a satire if he didn't give him the javelin. Cú Chulainn fired the javelin clean through his head.

'That was a dear and speedy gift,' said the satirist.

Hence the name Áth Tolam Sét, the Ford of the Speedy Gift. The copper point of the javelin landed at another ford further east. Umarrith, the Copper Landing Place, is the name of that ford.

Here is the list of those killed by Cú Chulainn in Cuib: Nath Coirpre at the grove named after him; Cruthan at his ford; the Cattlemen's Sons at their cairn; Marc on his hillock; Meille on his mound; Badb in his tower; and Bogaine in his bog.

Cú Chulainn turned again to Muirthemne, his heart set on defending his homeland. After going there he killed the Crónech men at Focherd. He came upon them as they were setting up camp. There were twenty of them, ten cupbearers and ten warriors.

Medb turned back again from the north after a fortnight's ravaging the province, attacking, among others, Findmór wife of Celtchar Mac Uthidir, and taking fifty of her women at the razing of Dún Sobairche in the Dál Riada country. Wherever in Cuib Medb rested her horsewhip, that place is known as Bile Medba, Medb's Mast.[3] Any ford or any high place that she stopped at is called Áth Medba, Medb's Ford, and Dindgna Medba, Medb's High Place.

They all met up again at Focherd, Ailill and Medb and the team that drove the bull. The bull's original keeper tried to make off with it, but by beating sticks on their shields they drove the bull into a narrow pass. There the hooves of the animals drove the keeper into the ground. Forgaimen – the Skin Rug – was his name. His remains are still there. And the hill there is called Forgaimen.

The problem that they slept with that night was where to find a man to stand against Cú Chulainn at the ford.

'Let's ask Cú Chulainn for a truce,' said Ailill.

'Lugaid's the man for the job,' said they all.

Lugaid went to speak with him.

The message was delivered.

'You can have your truce,' said Cú Chulainn, 'so long as you don't break it.'

Then they sent for Cúr Mac Dalath to take on Cú Chulainn. Anyone that Cúr drew blood from never lasted longer than nine days.

'If he kills Cú Chulainn,' said Medb, 'we win. If it's he who ends up getting killed, it will be a relief to us all. It's not pleasant being around him feeding or sleeping.'

Cúr arrived. He was far from pleased when he saw he was to meet a beardless youngster.

'This is some assignment you've given me, and no mistake,' he said. 'If I'd known this was the one I'd to fight I wouldn't have bothered to come. One of our own cubs would have done rightly.'

'On the contrary,' said Cormac Connlongas, 'we'd think it an achievement if you beat him yourself.'

'Well, things being what they are,' said Cúr, 'and since I said I'd do it, you can get ready to set off tomorrow morning, for it won't take me long to kill this young buck.'

Early the next morning he went to meet him, telling the army to prepare to advance after his encounter with Cú Chulainn, for they'd have a clear road.

He arrived to find Cú Chulainn practising his feats of arms.

Here is the list of his feats:[4] the ball-feat, the blade-feat and the feat of the levelled shield; the javelin-feat and the rope-feat; the body-feat, the cat-feat and the hero's salmon-leap; the pole-vault and the hurdle-leap; the noble charioteer's reverse turn; the *gae bolga* and the brazen edge; the wheel-feat and the eight-man-feat; the breathing-feat, the mouth-rage and the warrior's roar; the stop-cut and the ricochet-stun-shot; and climbing a spear and straightening up on its point. All these were performed according to warrior's rules.

For a third of the day Cúr threw everything he had against him from behind his shield, but failed to penetrate the whirlwind of Cú Chulainn's feats. In fact Cú Chulainn didn't even know he was under fire until Fiacha Mac Fir Febe said to him:

'Look out, there's a man attacking you!'

Cú Chulainn glanced up. He was still holding a ball from the ball-feat and he threw it so hard at Cúr that it ricocheted off the boss of his shield between rim and frame and out the back of the wretch's head.

Fergus went back to the army.

'You are bound by the terms of the truce,' he said, 'to wait here another day.'

'Not exactly here,' said Ailill. 'We'll go back to camp.'

Then Láth Mac Dabró was likewise put forward to face Cú Chulainn. He too fell. Again Fergus went back to remind them of their truce. So they stayed where they were, as Cúr Mac Dalath was killed, and Lath Mac Dabró, and Foirc Mac Trí n-Aignech, and Srubgaile Mac Eobith – all slain in single combat.

'Go to the camp, comrade Láeg,' said Cú Chulainn, 'and ask Lugaid Mac Nóis Uí Lomairc who is to take me on tomorrow. Get all the detail, and give him my warm regards.'

Láeg went.

'Well met,' said Lugaid. 'It's a hard station for Cú Chulainn, to be fighting the men of Ireland single-handed.'

'Who takes him on tomorrow?'

'Someone who is a comrade of both Cú Chulainn's and mine – bad cess to him and his weapons! – is taking him on:

Fer Báeth.[5] They said they'd give him Finnabair for it, and make him king of his people.'

Láeg went back to Cú Chulainn.

'My comrade Láeg does not seemed pleased with his news,' said Cú Chulainn.

Láeg gave him the whole story. Fer Báeth had been summoned to Ailill's and Medb's tent and told to sit down beside Finnabair. He was told she would be given to him on account of his being chosen to engage with Cú Chulainn. They considered him a strong contender because both he and Cú Chulainn had received the same training under Scáthach. They got him drunk on wine, telling him it showed how much they valued him, for they'd brought only fifty wagonloads of it with them. And Finnabair herself served him the dear wine.

'I don't hold with all this,' said Fer Báeth. 'Cú Chulainn is my foster-brother. Our lives are sworn to each other. But having said that, I could take him on tomorrow and cut off his head.'

'That you will,' said Medb.

Cú Chulainn sent Láeg to ask Lugaid to come and talk with him. Lugaid came.

'So Fer Báeth is coming to take me on tomorrow,' said Cú Chulainn.

'That he is,' said Lugaid.

'An evil day,' said Cú Chulainn. 'I won't come out of this alive. We are perfectly matched as regards age, skill and weight. Lugaid, give him my best wishes. Tell him that to take me on is not the act of a true warrior. Ask him to come and talk with me tonight.'

Lugaid spoke to him. Fer Báeth did not shirk the issue, but went that night with Fiacha Mac Fir Febe to renounce his friendship with Cú Chulainn. Cú Chulainn appealed to him as a foster-brother, brought up by the same foster-mother Scáthach.

'I'm obliged to do it,' said Fer Báeth. 'I gave Medb my word.'

'Then keep your friendship,' said Cú Chulainn, and he stormed off. In the glen he trod on a piece of split holly and the point came out at his knee. He pulled it out.

'Hold on, Fer Báeth, till you see what I've found.'

'Throw it over here,' said Fer Báeth.

Cú Chulainn threw the holly-rod after Fer Báeth. It went through the hollow at the back of his neck and out through his mouth, and he fell on his back in the glen.

'Some throw,' said Fer Báeth.

Hence the name Focherd – the Throw – in Muirthemne.

Or else it was Fiacha Mac Fir Febe who said: 'You were quick to throw today, Cú Chulainn,' and that thus Focherd was named.

'Your partner has fallen,' said Fergus. 'Tell me, will you have to pay for him tomorrow?'

'Whatever it takes,' said Cú Chulainn.

He sent Láeg again to see how matters stood in the camp, and whether Fer Báeth had survived. Said Lugaid:

'Fer Báeth has died. Tell Cú Chulainn to come and talk to me when he's ready.'

Then Fergus was heard to chant:

> Fer Báeth, your foolish foray
> led to a grave in this ground.
> You angered a wise fellow
> and found death in Croen Corand.
>
> In Croen Corand this high hill
> was called Fríthi from of old.
> But Fer Báeth, since here you fell
> Focherd shall it now be called.

'You'll have to get someone to fight him tomorrow,' said Lugaid.

'We'll get no one,' said Ailill, 'unless we're crafty. Any man that comes to you, give him wine till he's in good form, and say to him, "That's the last of the wine we brought from Crúachan, but we'd hate for you to have to drink water while you're in our camp" – and let Finnabair sit at his right hand, and then say to him, "You can have her if you bring back the head of the Torqued Man.'"

Each night a hero was sent for; each night the offer was made; and each hero in turn was killed. They were running out of heroes to take him on. So they called in Lugaid's brother, Láríne Mac Nóis. He had a great conceit of himself. They gave him wine and put Finnabair at his right hand. Medb looked at the pair.

'What a sweet couple,' she said, 'and so well matched.'

'I wouldn't argue with that,' said Ailill, 'and he shall have her if he brings me the head of the Torqued Man.'

'That I will,' said Láríne.

Lugaid approached them.

'Who have you got for the ford tomorrow?'

'Láríne's taken it on,' said Ailill.

Lugaid went to talk to Cú Chulainn. They met at Fer Báeth's Glen and saluted each other.

'Here's why I wanted to talk,' said Lugaid. 'They've got this thick-witted, arrogant boor – my brother Láríne. They tricked him with the girl. For the sake of our friendship don't kill him and leave me without a brother. He's been set up to set us two at odds. But I don't mind if you give him a good hiding, for he's coming despite me.'

The following day Láríne came to take on Cú Chulainn, with the girl there to cheer him on. Cú Chulainn went for him with his bare hands and forcibly disarmed him. Then he grabbed him and shook him and squeezed him till the shit ran out of him, polluting the ford and stinking up the air all around. Cú Chulainn threw him into Lugaid's arms. For the rest of his days his bowels didn't work right. He was never without chest trouble, and eating was a constant pain. Yet he is the only man who met Cú Chulainn on the Táin Bó

Cúailnge and escaped with his life – not that it was much of a life.

Cú Chulainn saw a young woman[6] coming towards him, very beautiful and wearing a dress of many colours.

'Who are you?' he said.

'The daughter of King Búan the Constant,' she said, 'and I've come to you. I love you because of all the things I've heard about you, and I've brought my treasures and my cattle with me.'

'This is not a good time,' said Cú Chulainn. 'We suffer failure and famine. It wouldn't be right for me to go with a woman, in the midst of such troubles.'

'I could be a help to you.'

'It wasn't for a woman's arse that I took this on.'

'Then I'll add to your troubles,' said she. 'I'll go for you when you're deep into fighting. I'll get under your feet in the ford in the shape of an eel and make sure you fall.'

'That's easier to swallow than the king's daughter,' he said. 'I'll get you between my toes and I'll break your ribs, and you'll bear that mark forever unless it's lifted from you by a blessing.'

'I'll come as a grey she-wolf, and stampede cattle into the ford against you.'

'I'll put your eye out with a stone from my sling, and you'll bear that mark forever unless it's lifted from you by a blessing.'

'I'll come as a hornless red heifer, and lead the cattle to surge against you in the waters, whether ford or pool, and you'll not know me.'

'I'll fire a stone at you,' he said, 'and break the leg from under you, and you'll bear that mark forever unless it's lifted from you by a blessing.'

She left him then.

Lóch[7] Mac Emonis was the next to be called up. They promised him Finnabair, a piece of the arable land of Aí as big as Muirthemne Plain, gear for a dozen soldiers and a chariot worth seven bondmaids. But he thought it beneath him to fight a mere boy. He had a brother, Long[8] Mac Emonis, and they offered him the same bounty – girl, gear, chariot and land. He went to meet Cú Chulainn. Cú Chulainn killed him and had the body sent to his brother Lóch. Lóch said that if he knew it was a grown man who had killed him, he would kill him for it.

That day, Cú Chulainn put on his festive garb, and the women climbed on the men's shoulders to catch a glimpse of him. They called out to him that he was being mocked in the camp because he had no beard, and that a real warrior wouldn't fight him, only little imps like himself, and he'd be better off putting on a false beard. So he did, in order to get Lóch to fight him. He took a fistful of grass and whispered a spell into it to make them all think he had a beard.

'True enough,' said the women. 'Cú Chulainn has a beard. Now it's right and proper for a warrior to take him on.'

They did this in order to get Lóch to fight him, but Lóch said:

'I won't fight him until tomorrow week.'

'It's not right and proper to leave him in peace for that length of time,' said Medb. 'We'll send a squad of heroes every night to seek him out and catch him off guard.'

They did so: a squad went every night to seek him out, and he killed them all. He killed seven Conalls, seven Oenguses, seven Uarguses, seven Celtres, eight Fiacs, ten Ailills, ten Delbaeths and ten Tasachs. Such were his accomplishments that week in Áth Grena.

So Medb began to pressurize Lóch.

'It's a great shame on you,' she said, 'that your brother's murderer is wreaking havoc on our army, and you're not fit to take him on. Surely a jumped-up little imp like him would be no match for the fire and fury of a warrior like you, and anyway, didn't the same foster-mother teach you the same martial arts?'

Lóch went to avenge his brother, persuaded that he would meet a bearded man.

'Come to the ford upstream,' said Lóch. 'I'll not meet you in a ford tainted by my brother's death.'

As Cú Chulainn came to the ford some men were driving cattle over it.

'There'll be a thirst for water at the ford today,' said Gabrán the poet.

Hence the names Áth Tarteisc,[9] Ford of the Thirst for Water, and Tír Mór Tarteisc, the Hinterland of Tarteisc.

As the men clashed in the ford, jabbing and slashing at each other, an eel cast three coils about Cú Chulainn's feet and threw him on to his back. Lóch attacked him with his sword till the ford ran red with his blood.

'This is a poor show,' said Fergus, 'to put on before the enemy. Someone heckle him, otherwise it'll be no contest.'

Bricriu 'Venom Tongue' Mac Carbada got to his feet and began to heckle Cú Chulainn.

'You're finished!' he said, 'losing out to a small fish just as the men of Ulster struggle from their sick-beds to help you. But then it must be hard for you to act the champion when you're up against a real contender, with all of Ireland looking on.'

With that, Cú Chulainn got up and lashed out at the eel and broke its ribs, and so thunderous was the combat of the two heroes that the cattle ran amok east through the army and carried off their tents on their horns.

Then a she-wolf attacked him and drove the cattle back westwards against him. He fired a stone from his sling at her that put out the eye in her head.

She came in the shape of a hornless red heifer and led the cattle stampeding through the fords and pools. And he said:

'I can't see the ford for water!'

He fired a stone at the heifer and broke the leg from under her.

Then he turned to Lóch and assaulted him with the barbed *gae bolga* Láeg had sent downstream to him. He thrust it up through the rear portal[10] of Lóch's body, for when Lóch was fighting, the rest of him was covered by a skin of horn.

'Grant me one favour,' said Lóch. 'I don't ask for quarter like a coward. Yield me one step and let me stand up so I can fall forward to the east, for if I fall back to the west, the men of Ireland will think I've yielded to you.'

'Granted,' said Cú Chulainn. 'It is a warrior's request.'

He stepped back and Lóch fell forward on his face. Cú Chulainn cut off his head.

Hence the name Áth Traiged – the Ford of the Step – in Tír Mór.

Then a great weariness descended on Cú Chulainn, and he chanted this verse:

> I am alone against hordes
> I cannot stop nor let go.
> I stand here in the long cold hours
> alone against every foe.
>
> Tell Conchobar he must come now
> to help in this hour of need.
> Mágach's sons have taken our cows
> to divide among their breed.
>
> In my fight I have been free
> but one stick will not make fire.
> Had I only two or three,
> then there'd be a blaze indeed.
>
> I am almost worn out
> by much fighting one on one.
> Their best soldiers make me doubt
> if I can stand here alone.

The Morrígan appeared to him in the shape of a one-eyed old hag, milking a cow with three teats. He was dying with thirst, and he asked her for a drink. She gave him milk from the first teat.

'Good health to the giver,' said Cú Chulainn, 'and the blessings of the gods of heaven and earth on you!'

With that, her ribs were healed.

She gave him milk from the second teat, and her eye was healed.

She gave him milk from the third teat, and her leg was healed.

'You told me once,' she said, 'that you would never heal me.'

'Had I known it was you,' said Cú Chulainn, 'I never would have.'

'Let's ask Cú Chulainn for a truce,' said Ailill and Medb.

Lugaid went to him and Cú Chulainn granted the truce.

'But have a man at the ford for me tomorrow,' said Cú Chulainn.

Medb had six hired princes in her private army, heirs to the royal family of Clann Dedad – the Three Dark-Haired Men of Imlech, and the Three Red-Headed Men of Sruthair.

'Why don't we gang up on Cú Chulainn?' they said.

They ganged up on Cú Chulainn and Cú Chulainn killed the six of them.

Again Medb pondered what to do about Cú Chulainn. She was greatly pained by the number of casualties being inflicted by him on her army. She decided to seek a meeting with him on the pretext of negotiating a peace, and to have a gang of armed and dangerous men lying in wait there to overpower and apprehend him. She sent a messenger – Traigthrén, the Powerful Foot – asking Cú Chulainn to meet her, and to come unarmed, as she would be accompanied only by her retinue of women. Cú Chulainn undertook to do so.

'Cú Chulainn,' said Láeg, 'how do you intend to approach this meeting tomorrow?'

'As Medb requested,' said Cú Chulainn.

'Medb's resources are many,' said the charioteer. 'Beware the hand behind her back.'

'So how should I approach it?' said Cú Chulainn.

'With your sword at your hip,' said the charioteer, 'in case of ambush. A warrior without weapons has no recourse to a warrior's compensation, but is worth only the paltry price of a non-combatant.'

'Let it be done as you say,' said Cú Chulainn.

The meeting was in Ard Aignech, the Height of the Fleet Horses, known as Focherd today. Medb came and set a trap for Cú Chulainn with fourteen of the most formidable men in her personal guard – two called Glas Sinna, both sons of Briccride; two called Ardán, both sons of Lecc; two called Glas Ogma, both sons of Cronn; and Drúcht and Delt and Daithen and Téa and Tascur and Tualang and Taur and Glese.

Cú Chulainn came to meet Medb. The men jumped out at him. Fourteen javelins were thrown at him simultaneously, but he dodged them so that neither hide nor hair of him was harmed. Then he went for them and killed the fourteen of them. These are the Focherd Fourteen, also known as the Casualties of Crónech, for they met their death at Crónech in Focherd.

Then Cú Chulainn chanted:

> this great deed of mine outshines
> the brilliant spectral army
> thunderstruck by my attack
> lightning is the war I wage
> against the hidden squadrons
> likewise Ailill likewise Medb
> unfostering their dark arts
> through women conspirators
> who stalk with cold treachery
> over the true warrior
> and his words of brave advice
> that shine all the more brilliant
> because of his true deeds

Some say that it was after this 'great deed' – *fó-cherd* – that
Focherd was named.

Then Cú Chulainn encountered the army as they were setting up camp and he killed two men called Daigre, two called
Anle and four Dungaises of Imlech. On the same day the
rules of fair fight were broken against him when he was
attacked by a gang of five consisting of two Crúaids, two
Calads and a Derethor. Cú Chulainn killed them single-
handed.

Fergus declared that there must be no more foul play. So
they came to meet Cú Chulainn in single combat and in this
manner he killed another five at Dún Cinn Coros, now called
Delga, the Spike, in Muirthemne. Then he killed Fota in the
field named after him, Bó Mailce on his ford, Salach in his
marsh, Muinne in his ford, Luath in Lethbara and Fer Tóithle
in Tóithle. So wherever these men were killed their names
have survived them. Cú Chulainn killed Traig, Dorn and
Derna – Foot, Fist and Palm – and Col, Mebal and Eraise –
Lust, Shame and Trash – on this side of the ford of Tír
Mór at Méithe and Cethe. These were three druids and their
consorts.

After this Medb sent a hundred men from her private army
to kill Cú Chulainn. He killed them all at Áth Chéit Chúile –
the Ford of the Crime of the One Hundred. It was here that
Medb said: 'It's a crime, the way our people are being killed.'
Hence also the names Glais Chró – the Bloody Stream – and
Cuilenn Cinn Dúin – the Crime at the Head of the Fort.

Then he kept raining stones on them from the heights of
Delga so that no living thing, man or beast, dared put its head
past him southwards between Delga and the sea.


'Bring him this offer,' said Ailill: 'he can have Finnabair, if he
leaves our army alone.'

Maine Athramail the Fatherlike went to him. He met his
charioteer Láeg.

'Whom do you serve under?' he said.

Láeg made no reply. Maine asked him the same thing three times.

'I serve under Cú Chulainn,' he said, 'and stop pestering me or I'll take your head off.'

'What an ill-tempered fellow,' said Maine, and turned from him.

So he went to speak to Cú Chulainn. Cú Chulainn had taken off his shirt and was sitting waist-deep in the snow, except the snow had melted a man's length around him from the heat of his warrior's body. Maine asked him three times whom he served under.

'I serve under Conchobar,' he said, 'and stop pestering me. If you keep on pestering me I'll take off your head like a blackbird's.'

'It's not easy talking with these two,' said Maine.

So he left then, and told Ailill and Medb what had happened.

'Let Lugaid go,' said Ailill, 'and offer him the girl.'

So Lugaid went and gave him the message.

'Comrade Lugaid,' said Cú Chulainn, 'this is a trick.'

'It's the word of a king,' said Lugaid. 'It's no trick.'

'Let's do it, so,' said Cú Chulainn.

Lugaid went and gave Cú Chulainn's answer to Ailill and Medb.

'Let my fool go as me,' said Ailill, 'with a king's crown on his head. Get him to stand at a distance from Cú Chulainn so that he won't be recognized. He can take the girl with him, hand her over to Cú Chulainn, and leave them to it. Very likely Cú Chulainn will be distracted long enough not to bother us until such times as he joins up with the Ulstermen for the final battle.'

So the fool – his name was Tamun, the Stump – went to Cú Chulainn with the girl and spoke to him from a distance. Cú Chulainn knew from the way he spoke that he was a fool. He was carrying a sling-stone in his hand and he threw it at him. It penetrated the fool's head and knocked his brains out.

Cú Chulainn went up to the girl and cut off her two plaits and thrust a pillar-stone through her cloak and her tunic. He thrust another pillar-stone through the fool's middle. Their standing stones are still there, Finnabair's Stone and the Fool's Stone. Cú Chulainn left them like that.

Ailill and Medb sent out a search party for them because they'd been away so long. They were found as they were. The story spread throughout the camp. After that there was no further truce between them and Cú Chulainn.

# VIII
# THE GREAT SLAUGHTER

THE FOUR PROVINCES of Ireland set up a fortified camp in Muirthemne at Breslech Mór, Great Slaughter. They consigned their cattle and plunder southwards to Clithar Bó Ulad, the Ulster Cattle-Shelter. Cú Chulainn took up a position nearby at the mound of Lerga, and as dusk fell his charioteer Láeg Mac Riangabra, Son of the Horse-road, lit a fire for him. Off in the distance he could see, above the heads of the allied army, the fiery flickering of their golden weapons as the sun set in the evening clouds. A terrible rage filled him at the sight of that immense army, the enormous number of his enemies. He seized his two spears and his shield and his sword. He shook the shield and brandished the spears and waved the sword, and flung forth his warrior's roar from deep in his throat so that the goblins and ghouls and sprites of the glen and the fiends of the air gave answer, so fearsome was his utterance. Then the Nemain threw the army into confusion. The spear-points and weapons of the allied army clashed tumultuously and a hundred warriors fell dead as their hearts burst with terror in the middle of the camp and on the ramparts that night.

From where he stood Láeg saw a lone man crossing the camp, coming towards them from the north-east.

'A lone man approaches, Little Cú,' said Láeg.

'What kind of man?' said Cú Chulainn.

'In brief, he's a tall, good-looking man. He has a square-cut beard. Curly yellow hair. He wears a green cloak pinned to

his breast with a bright silver brooch. Next to his white skin,
a knee-length tunic of royal satin embroidered with red gold.
He carries a black shield with a boss of white bronze, a
five-pointed spear and a forked javelin. He whirls them about
him in a display of spectacular skill, yet no one challenges
him, and he takes no one under his notice, as if they couldn't
see him.'

'Nor can they, my young friend,' said Cú Chulainn. 'This
is a friendly being come from the other world to offer me
support, for they know the hardship I undergo as I fight alone
on the Táin Bó Cúailnge against the four provinces of Ireland.'

It was indeed as Cú Chulainn had said. When the warrior
arrived, he commiserated with him.

'This is brave work, Cú Chulainn,' he said.

'It's nothing much,' said Cú Chulainn.

'I shall help you now,' said the warrior.

'Who exactly are you?' said Cú Chulainn.

'I am Lug Mac Ethlenn,[1] your father in the other world.'

'My wounds are serious. It's time they were healed.'

'Sleep now for a while, Cú Chulainn,' said the warrior, 'a
deep sleep of three days and three nights here on the mound
of Lerga, and I'll withstand the army for that time.'

His guardian sang him a low melody until he fell asleep,
and he looked over his wounds, and saw to it that they were
clean. Then Lug chanted:

> rise mighty son of Ulster
> now that your wounds have been healed
> a fair man facing your foes
> in the starlit ford of night
> against the onslaught of spears
> as multitudes are laid low
> aided by the other world
> to watch over your domain
> with forceful integrity
> as you stand guard all alone

defending wandering herds
to kill the ghosts that I kill
their life in this world is not long
so wreak fury and havoc on
your faltering enemies
leap into your chariot
and then arise

For three days and three nights Cú Chulainn slept, as well he might, for his sleep was as deep as his wounds. From the Monday after Samain[2] until the Wednesday after Imbolc,[3] Cú Chulainn had not slept, except in brief snatches after midday, leaning against his spear with head on fist and fist on spear and spear on knee, so deeply was he into slashing and stabbing and slaughtering and scything down the four great provinces of Ireland.

Then the warrior from the other world applied healing herbs to Cú Chulainn's wounds – cuts, hacks, gashes, bruises – so that he recovered in his sleep without knowing it.

As he slept, the young fellows in Emain discussed what was going on.

'It's a crying shame,' they said, 'that Cú Chulainn has no one to help him.'

'Let me ask you this,' said Follomain the son of Conchobar: 'do I have a company of fellows who will follow me to help him?'

Three fifties of young fellows shouldered their hurleys and set off with him. The army saw them coming across the plain.

'A body of men is advancing towards us,' said Ailill.

Fergus went to look.

'These are some of the young fellows of Ulster,' he said, 'coming to help Cú Chulainn.'

'Send out an armed force to engage them,' said Ailill, 'and don't let Cú Chulainn know about it, for if they join up with him, there'll be no beating them.'

A detachment of soldiers went out to meet them. Three

times the young fellows fought the army, and killed three
times their own number, but at the end of that encounter
at Lia Toll, the Hole-Stone, not one remained alive except
Follomain the son of Conchobar. Follomain swore he would
never go back to Emain unless he took Ailill's head with him
accompanied by its gold crown. But that was easier sworn
than done: the two sons of Beithe Mac Báin, sons of Ailill's
foster-parents, tracked him down and attacked him, and he
died at their hands.

Meanwhile Cú Chulainn was sleeping the sleep of the just
for three days and three nights at the mound of Lerga. Then
he rose from his slumber and passed his hand over his face
and turned crimson from head to foot: he felt strong and
energetic, fit for a market day, or a march, or female company,
or a drinking-bout, or one of the great assemblies of Ireland.

'Warrior!' said Cú Chulainn. 'How long have I been asleep?'

'For three days and three nights,' said the warrior.

'More's the pity,' said Cú Chulainn.

'Why so?' said the warrior.

'The army has been free from attack all that time,' said Cú
Chulainn.

'Not so,' said the warrior.

'Why then, who attacked them?' said Cú Chulainn.

'The young fellows came south from Emain Macha, three
fifties of them, sons of the kings of Ulster, led by Follomain
the son of Conchobar. For the three days you were asleep
they fought the army three times, and killed three times their
own number, but not one of them survived except Follomain.
And Follomain swore to take Ailill's head, but that was easier
sworn than done, for in the end he too was killed.'

'Then it's a terrible pity I hadn't my strength,' said Cú
Chulainn, 'for had I been fit, the young fellows would not
have been killed, and Follomain the son of Conchobar would
still be alive.'

'Keep up the good fight, Little Cú; there's no stain on your
honour, no disgrace on your valour.'

'Stay with us tonight,' said Cú Chulainn, 'and together we may avenge the death of the boys.'

'I will not stay,' said the warrior, 'for no matter what great deeds of courage a man does in your company, the glory and the fame and reputation will be yours, not his. So I will not stay. Take the fight to the army by yourself, for they have no power over your life at this time.'

'The scythed chariot, comrade Láeg!' said Cú Chulainn. 'Can you get her geared up and ready to go? If that's the case, let's drive, and if not, don't bother.'

The charioteer sprang to his feet and put on his charioteer's battle-garb. This was the outfit: first, the sleek deerskin tunic, soft and light as air, supple and smoothly tailored for maximum arm-movement. Over that, the cloak of raven's-plumage black, which Simon Magus had made for Darius the king of the Romans, and which Darius had given to Conchobar, and Conchobar to Cú Chulainn, and Cú Chulainn to Láeg. Next, the plated, four-cornered, crested helmet, richly coloured and crafted, so perfectly poised on his shoulders as to seem weightless. With his two hands he adjusted the deep yellow headband to glow on his brow like a strip of red gold beaten out on an anvil's edge; this was the badge that distinguished him from his master. He decked out the horses in their damascened armour, covering them from head to hoof with steel plate spiked with blades, tangs and spear-points; as for the chariot itself, it bristled at every angle and corner, front and rear, so that anywhere the vehicle moved it brought a lacerating edge to bear. He took the long whip and the ornamented goad in his right hand; his left hand grasped the reins that controlled the steeds. Then he cast a cloaking spell over them and his companion, rendering them invisible to all within the camp, while all remained visible to them. Under cover of that spell the charioteer could best exploit his special skills on the day – the snap jump, the frontal assault and the slalom at full speed.

Then the great hero Cú Chulainn son of Sualdam, builder

of the Badb's palisade of human bodies, put on his warrior's battle-garb. This was the outfit: first, the twenty-seven corsets of waxed skin, stiffened, compact, board-like, hooped to his own fair skin with drawstrings, ropes and cables to prevent his inner being and his brain from breaking loose at the onset of his fury. Over these he fastened the battle-girdle of hard, tough, tanned leather cut from the choicest parts of seven yearling ox-hides, covering him from slender waist to the breadth between armpits; this he wore to repel spears, pikes, lances, darts and arrows, which glanced off as if they'd struck rock or horn. Then he slipped on the apron of filmy silk with its variegated white bronze border over his soft underbelly. Over the apron of filmy silk, the dark apron of pliable oxblood leather cut from four yearling ox-hides, battle-belted with a thick strap of cowhide.

Then the beautiful champion took up his weapons of contest and warfare and strife. These were the weapons he picked: eight short swords with the gleaming bone-hilted sword; eight little spears with the five-pronged spear; eight light javelins with the bone-hilted javelin; eight small darts with the barbed dart known as the Riddling-Rod; eight double-dealing shields with the oxblood-red curved shield that could cup a prize boar in its bowl, its rim so razor-sharp it could cut a hair against the current. When the warrior performed the double-deal of the shield-rim, he could slice as keenly as with sword or spear. Then he placed on his head the battle-hardened war-helmet from whose ridges and chambers his roar of a hundred warriors reverberated, echoed by the goblins and ghouls and sprites of the glen and the fiends of the air, for their howls would resound before him, above him and around him any time he went forth to shed the blood of warriors and heroes. He drew about him his cloak of invisibility made of cloth from Tír Tairngire, the Land of Promise, and given to him by his foster-father in the dark arts.

The first Torque seized Cú Chulainn and turned him into a contorted thing, unrecognizably horrible and grotesque.

Every slab and every sinew of him, joint and muscle, shuddered from head to foot like a tree in the storm or a reed in the stream. His body revolved furiously inside his skin. His feet and his shins and his knees jumped to the back; his heels and his calves and his hams to the front. The bunched sinews of his calves jumped to the front of his shins, bulging with knots the size of a warrior's clenched fist. The ropes of his neck rippled from ear to nape in immense, monstrous, incalculable knobs, each as big as the head of a month-old child.

Then he made a red cauldron of his face and features: he sucked one of his eyes so deep into his head that a wild crane would find it difficult to plumb the depths of his skull to drag that eye back to its socket; the other popped out on to his cheek. His mouth became a terrifying, twisted grin. His cheek peeled back from his jaws so you could see lungs and liver flapping in his throat; lower and upper palate clashed like a pair of mighty tongs, and a stream of white-hot flecks broad as a ram's fleece poured from his mouth. His heart belled against his ribs like a bloodhound guldering for its food, or a lion roaring through bears. The clouds that boiled above him in his fury glimmered and flickered with malignant flares and sultry smoke – the torches of the Badb. His hair became the wiry tangle of a red thornbush that fences a gap in a stone wall. If a royal apple-tree laden with regal fruit were shaken over his head, hardly an apple would reach the ground, but would find itself spiked by a strand of his hair as it bristled with rage. The hero's light sprang from his forehead, long and thick as a warrior's whetstone, long as a prow, and he clattered with rage as he wielded the shields, urging his charioteer on and raining stones on the massed army. Then thick, steady, strong, high as the mast of a tall ship was the straight spout of dark blood that rose up from the fount of his skull to dissolve in an otherworldly mist like the smoke that hangs above a royal hunting-lodge when a king comes to be looked after at the close of a winter's day.

Transformed by the Torque, the hero Cú Chulainn sprang

into his scythed chariot that glittered with iron tangs, blades,
hooks, hard prongs and brutal spikes, barbs and sharp nails
on every shaft, strut, strap and truss. The chariot was built
on sleek, spare lines, arrowy and high-sprung, with space for
a lordly warrior's eightfold weapons, and drove like a swallow
or the wind or a deer over the level plain. The chariot was
hitched to a pair of fast, furious, eager-headed, able-bodied
horses, slender-eared and roan-breasted, keen and confident
in harness, lovely to look at between the trim shafts. One
horse was lithe and swift-leaping, battle-ready, arched and
powerful, long in body and broad in hoof. The other flowing-
maned, slight and slender, shining in hoof and heel.

He came out fighting with the thunder-feat of one hundred,
and the thunder-feat of two hundred, and of three hundred,
and of four hundred, and of five hundred, at which point he
paused, thinking that would do rightly for the first round of
the first bout of his battle with the four provinces of Ireland.
Then, to show his great hatred of them, he brought the chariot
in a great circle round the provinces of Ireland, driving so
hard that the iron tyres ploughed deep into the ground and
threw up a bank of earth the height of the wheels, with clods,
boulders, rocks, flagstones and gravel enough for the outer
rampart of an armed camp. He made that wall of the Badb
round the four great provinces of Ireland so as not to have
his enemies escape and scatter, but to hold them close to him
and thus to wreak vengeance for the death of the young
fellows of Ulster. He drove into their packed ranks, an enemy
to beat all enemies, three times encircling them with great
ramparts of their own corpses piled sole to sole and headless
neck to headless neck, so all-encompassing was the carnage.
Three times again he circled them, leaving a layer of them six
deep, the soles of three to the necks of three in a ring-fence
round the camp. So that the name of this episode in the *Táin*
is Seisrech Breslige, the Sixfold Slaughter. It is one of the three
massacres in the *Táin* whose casualties are beyond computation: Seisrech Breslige, Imshlige Glennamnach – the Mutual

Slaughter of Glenamnach – and the Battle of Gáirech and Ilgáirech. Though, on this occasion, horses and dogs could be reckoned as well as men. No body-count was made of the common soldiery, so we have no way of knowing how many died in total. Only their leaders were accounted for. These are the names of their chiefs and commanders: two Crúaids, two Calads, two Círs, two Cíars, two Ecells, three Croms, three Cauraths, three Combirges, four Feochars, four Furachars, four Casses, four Fotas, five other Cauraths, five Cermans, five Cobthachs, six Saxans, six Dáchs, six Dáires, seven Rochaids, seven Rónáns, seven Rúrthechs, eight Rochlads, eight Rochtads, eight Rindachs, eight Cairpres, eight Mulachs, nine Daigiths, nine other Dáires, nine Dámachs, ten Fiacs, ten Fiachas and ten Fedelmids.

In that great Massacre on Muirthemne Plain Cú Chulainn slew seven score and ten kings as well as innumerable dogs and horses, women and children, not to mention underlings and rabble; and not one man in three escaped without a staved head, or a broken leg, or a burst eye, or without being scarred for life in some other way. And Cú Chulainn came away from that encounter without so much as a scrape or scratch on himself, or his man, or his horses.

Cú Chulainn emerged the next morning to survey the enemy and to display his elegant figure to matrons and maidens and young girls and poets and practitioners of verse, for he deemed neither dignified nor seemly the nightmarish form in which he had appeared the night before. So he came to them by day to let them see his true beauty. Gorgeous indeed was Cú Chulainn Mac Sualdaim as he paraded himself before what was left of the army. His hair was arranged in three layers: dark next to the scalp, blood-red in the middle, and yellow at the ends, which were set like a gold crown on his head, falling to the nape of the neck in a braid of three coils, with little ringlets and gold-shiny strands combed out in artful disarray about his shoulders. A hundred curls of purple gold shone

round his neck; a hundred amber-beaded ribbons bedecked
his head. He had four dimples in each cheek – yellow, green,
blue and purple. Seven brilliant gems gleamed in each regal
eye. Each foot had seven toes and each hand seven fingers,
the nails or claws or talons of each with the grip of a hawk
or a griffin. He had put on his festive garb for the day. This
was what he wore: a beautifully becoming purple mantle,
with a fringe of five folds, pinned over his white breast with
a silver brooch inlaid with filigree of gold, shining like a
lantern that is too bright to look at; and next to his skin, a
sheer silk tunic reaching down to the top of his warrior's
apron of royal satin. He carried an oxblood-red shield with
five concentric gold rings and a rim of white bronze. The
ornamented gold guard of his sword sat proud above his belt.
Nearby in the chariot stood a tall javelin with a gold-riveted
head and an edge of blued steel. He held nine human heads
in one hand, ten in the other. He waved them at the army.
These were Cú Chulainn's overnight trophies.

The women of Connacht climbed up on the men's shoulders
to get a glimpse of Cú Chulainn. Medb dared not show her
face for dread of him, and stayed where she was under her
tortoise-shell of shields. Then Dubthach Dóel, the Beetle of
Ulster, said this:

> If this be the Torqued Man, then
> many corpses will ensue,
> cries resound in the walled courts,
> and tales that are all too true –
>
> headstones erected on graves,
> increased by the royal dead;
> not well do you bring the fight
> to this solitary blade.
>
> I see his malignant shape,
> the nine heads under his bed,

these prized possessions of his
our fragments, like these ten heads.

I see your women's faces
raised above the lines for him,
and I see that your great queen
dare not risk her life or limb.

Were you to take my advice,
your army would form a plan
to surround him and cut short
the reign of the Torqued Man.

And Fergus replied:

Consign Dubthach Beetle-Tongue
to the back of the army!
Nothing but harm has he done
since the young maidens were slain.[4]

Wicked the deed when he killed
Fiacha the son of Conchobar,
and worse again when he killed
Coirpre the son of Fedelmid.

Black Dubthach dare not contend
for the kingship of Ulster,
so this is how he uses men –
those not killed he sets at odds.

All the exiles would lament
the loss of their beardless son,
and Ulster will be hell-bent
on driving you like cattle,
your herds scattered far and wide
when the men of Ulster rise.

Messengers will bring great news
of great queens brought down to ground,
men's bodies violated
and piled up in a great mound.

Shields scattered on the dark slopes,
ravens tearing at dead meat,
corpses trampled underfoot,
human vultures at the feast.

Everywhere the dogs of war
will cause havoc when they can.
We exiles have wandered far
indeed from our Ulster land.
Dubthach heeds not what I say.
So take him away.

Fergus flung Dubthach from him and he ended up nose-down before a nearby troop of onlookers.

Then Ailill said:

enough of     your threats     Fergus
on account of     Ulster     cows and women
I know by     the gaps     that slaughter
will ensue     though singly     they die
by the ford     one day     at a time

Medb said:

rise up     Ailill     with your triple ranks
against the cattle     people     the boy
beguiling warrior     who shudders     by fords
who shatters     the dark pools     noble
Fergus     and his Ulster     exiles
when the war     is done     will get

> their dues     as they     pay back
> the poets     of heroic war

Fergus replied:

> close your ears     to crazy women
> flames blossoming     among kith     and unfaithful
> kin     unripe     as yet
> the counsel     of a king     of knowledge
> to be equal     in the secret act

The poet Gabrán said:

> leave off     your words     this queenly dross
> to strew     before her followers     sweet acorns
> for keen blades     to bring forth     what comes
> swelling fiercely from     the knob     of a shield

'Don't refuse the match,' said Fergus. 'Go and take him on at the ford.'
'Listen to Ailill,' said Medb.
Ailill said:

> Fergus knows     this people     all too well
> bleating followers     of cattle     but to drive
> cattle     with sharp goads     he swears
> to bring     them round     through the mist
> the long way     by the gap     of the brazen mouth

Fergus said:

> do not Medb     shear off     your exiles
> the full crop     of a year     fierce women
> squabbling over     the spoils     this man
> who came     to strive with     your followers

The loyal hero Fiacha Fíaldána Dimraith went to talk with his mother's sister's son, Maine Andóe the Quick Man. Dócha Mac Mágach came with Maine Andóe, and Dubthach the Beetle of Ulster came with Fiacha Fialdána. Dócha threw a spear at Fiacha and hit his companion Dubthach. At the same time Dubthach threw a spear at Fiacha and hit his cousin Dócha – the mothers of Dubthach and Dócha were sisters.

Hence the name Imroll Belaig Eóin, the Bad Throw at Bird Pass.

Or, according to another account, Imroll Belaig Eóin got its name later, when the Ulstermen had recovered from the Curse. The two armies had set up camp there when Diarmait, Conchobar's son, came south from Ulster.

'Let a horseman be sent,' said Diarmait, 'to tell Maine he can meet me, and we'll talk.'

So they met.

'I've come from Conchobar,' said Diarmait, 'to let Ailill and Medb know that if they return the cattle, the other damage will be overlooked; and let the bull from the east be brought to go head to head with our bull, since that was what Medb bargained for.'

'I'll go and tell them that,' said Maine.

So he went to Ailill and Medb.

'The terms don't suit Medb,' said Maine.

'Let's exchange weapons, then,' said Diarmait, 'if it's all right by you.'

'All right by me,' said Maine.

Each threw his spear towards the other and each killed the other. In this way Imroll Belaig Eóin, the Bad Throw at Bird Pass, got its name.

Then the two forces clashed. Three score fell on each side. Hence the name Ard in Dírma, Force Height.

A bold Ulster hero, Aengus son of Aenláime Gaibe the One-Handed, delayed the whole army at Moda Loga – Lug's Measure – as far as Áth Da Ferta, the Ford of the Two

Grave Mounds. He held them at bay by showering them with flagstones. Experts say that had the army accepted single combat with him, he would have beaten them before they came under the sword at Emain Macha. But the rules of fair fight were not upheld. He died fighting against the odds.

'Send out somebody to fight me,' said Cú Chulainn at the ford of Da Ferta.

'Not me! Anybody but me!' said everyone in turn. 'My family owes no dues. And even if they did, why should I be the scapegoat?'

Fergus Mac Róich was urged to take him on, but he refused to fight his foster-son Cú Chulainn. They plied him with wine till he was full drunk and again they urged him to go and fight him. He gave in under the pressure, and went.

'You must have been given some assurance,' said Cú Chulainn, 'to take me on with no sword in your scabbard.'

(For as we explained before, Ailill had stolen it.)

'Sword or no sword,' said Fergus, 'I wouldn't use it against you. Yield to me this once, Cú Chulainn.'

'If you yield to me some other time,' said Cú Chulainn.

'Done,' said Fergus.

Cú Chulainn retreated back from Fergus as far as Grellach Dollaid, the Doleful Swamp, so that Fergus might retreat before him when it came to the final battle.

Cú Chulainn made off into the swamp.

'After him, Fergus!' they all cried.

'Not this time,' said Fergus. 'It's not so easily managed. He's a quick one, that. I won't be going after him till my turn comes round again.'

They went on then and pitched camp in Crích Rois. Ferchú[5] Loingsech, who had been exiled by Ailill, heard what had happened and came to take on Cú Chulainn. He brought a squad of twelve men with him. Cú Chulainn killed them at Cingit Ferchon, Ferchú's Goblet. Thirteen gravestones mark the spot.

*

Medb sent Mand Muresci, the son of Dáire Domnannaig, to fight Cú Chulainn. Mand was a brother of Damán, Fer Diad's father. This Mand was an ugly customer, as fond of his grub as he was of his bed. He was as foul-mouthed as Dubthach the Beetle, as rough and ready of limb as Munremar Mac Gerrcinn the Thick-necked. He had the brute strength of Triscod, that pillar of Conchobar's household.

'I'll go for him unarmed, and crush him with my bare hands, for it's beneath me to use a weapon against such a barefaced whippersnapper.'

So Mand went out to find Cú Chulainn. Cú Chulainn and his charioteer were on the plain keeping a look-out for the army.

'A lone man approaches,' said Láeg.

'What kind of man?' said Cú Chulainn.

'A powerful big dark bull of a man, unarmed.'

'Let him come on,' said Cú Chulainn.

Mand came up to them.

'Are you looking for a fight? I am,' said Mand.

They grappled for a long time and Mand threw Cú Chulainn three times. The charioteer gave off to Cú Chulainn.

'If you were fighting for the champion's share in Emain,' he said, 'you'd make short work of the warriors there.'

Then his hero's rage and his fighting fury arose in Cú Chulainn. He tossed Mand against a nearby standing stone and smashed him to bits. Hence the name Mag Mandachta, that is, Mand Échta, the Plain of Mand's Death.

Then the men of Ireland debated who would best be able to take on Cú Chulainn the next morning. They all agreed it should be Calatín[6] Dána with his twenty-seven sons and his grandson Glas Mac Delga.[7] Every man of them had poison on him, and there was poison on all their weapons. They never missed a throw, and anyone they wounded, if he didn't die at once, died within nine days. They were promised a great bounty if they undertook the engagement; so they undertook it, and they shook hands on it. The contract was witnessed by Fergus, who had to agree: they argued that it should be considered single combat, since the sons of Calatín Dána were limb of his limb, flesh of his flesh, and that every issue of Calatín Dána's body was an extension of his body.

Fergus retired to his tent and his followers, and heaved a great sigh of weariness.

'I'm sickened by the deed that will be done tomorrow,' he said.

'What deed?' said his followers.

'The killing of Cú Chulainn,' he said.

'Never!' they said. 'Who's to kill him?'

'Calatín Dána,' he said, 'with his twenty-seven sons and Glas Mac Delga. Every man of them has poison on him, and there's poison on all their weapons, and anyone they wound, if he doesn't die at once, dies within nine days. And there is no man to whom I wouldn't give my weapons and my blessing, if he could go and witness that encounter, and tell me if Cú Chulainn should indeed be killed.'

'I'll go,' said Fiacha Mac Fir Febe.

They stayed there that night. Calatín Dána was up early the next morning with his twenty-seven sons and his grandson Glas Mac Delga. They set out to find Cú Chulainn. Fiacha Mac Fir Febe went after them. They found Cú Chulainn at the ford of Fuiliarn, and as one man they threw their twenty-nine spears at him, nor did they miss. Cú Chulainn did the 'blade-feat' with his shield and the spears sank half-way into it, so that though their aim was true, not one blade was reddened with his blood. Then Cú Chulainn drew his sword from its Badb's scabbard to lop off the weapons and so lighten his shield, but as he was doing so they all went for him and together they aimed their twenty-nine fists at his head. They beat him and hammered him down till his face met the sand and gravel of the ford. He gave out his warrior's roar and his cry of foul fight so that every living Ulsterman in the camp heard it, and anyone who didn't, he must have been asleep.

Then Fiacha Mac Fir Febe came on the scene. When he saw how things stood, he drew his sword from its Badb's scabbard and with one stroke he lopped off their twenty-nine fists, and they all fell backwards, so tight had been their grip.

Cú Chulainn raised his head and drew his breath and heaved a sigh of relief. Then he saw the man who had come to his aid.

'Well, foster-brother! A timely intervention!'

'Timely for you,' said Fiacha Mac Fir Febe, 'but not for us Ulster exiles, for if any one of them brings word of my little exploit back to the camp, all three thousand of our division will be put to the sword.'

'Upon my word,' said Cú Chulainn, 'now that I have drawn my breath, not one of them will live to tell the tale.'

With that, he went for them, slicing and hacking till their bodies were strewn in bits on all sides of the ford. One of them, Glas Mac Delga, took to his heels as Cú Chulainn was busy beheading the rest. Cú Chulainn sailed after him like a gust of wind. Glas reached Ailill and Medb's tent, but all he managed to say was 'Fiach . . .' before Cú Chulainn cut off his head.

'He made short work of that one, Fergus,' said Medb, 'but what was the debt (fiach) he spoke of?'

'I couldn't say,' said Fergus, 'unless someone in the camp owed him something, and it was preying on his mind. Whatever it was, it must have been a debt of flesh and blood. For by the same token, his debts have now been paid in full.'

So fell Calatín Dána the Bold at the hands of Cú Chulainn, together with his twenty-seven sons and his grandson Glas Mac Delga. In the bed of the ford is the stone round which they fought and struggled, and it still bears the marks of their sword-hilts, and their knees and elbows, and the butts of their spears. Their twenty-nine headstones were erected nearby. The name of the ford is Fuiliarn, downstream from Fer Diad's ford. And it is called Fuiliarn – Blood-Iron – because of the swords that were bloodied there.

# IX
# THE COMBAT
# OF
# CÚ CHULAINN
# AND
# FER DIAD

AGAIN THE MEN OF Ireland debated among themselves as to which man would be most capable of withstanding Cú Chulainn, and who should be next to go and face him at the ford. Finally they decided it should be the horn-skinned man from Irrus Domnann, that irresistible force, that indomitable rock of battle, Cú Chulainn's own dear devoted foster-brother. Cú Chulainn had no technique in his armoury that he couldn't match, except that of the *gae bolga*; and they thought he would withstand even that, for he had a covering of horn which no weapon or blade could pierce.

Medb sent messengers to Fer Diad.[1] They didn't come back with him. Medb sent poets and bards and satirists to flyte and mock and ridicule him; they said they would make three satires on him that would raise three blisters on his face – Shame, Stigma and Blot – so that there would be nowhere in the world where he could hold up his head, unless he came back to Ailill and Medb's tent on the Táin. Fer Diad came back with these emissaries, for fear of being put to shame by them.

Finnabair, the daughter of Ailill and Medb, was placed by his side. And Finnabair handed Fer Diad the goblets and the cups, and gave him three kisses with every cup, and held sweet fragrant apples at the cleavage of her tunic for him, saying that he was her only darling, her chosen lover from among all the men in the world.

When Fer Diad was well full and feeling good, Medb said:

'Well now, Fer Diad, do you know why you were invited to this tent?'

'Indeed I do not,' said Fer Diad, 'except that the noblest men in Ireland are here, and isn't it just right that I should be here too, with all these brave warriors?'

'Indeed that's not why,' said Medb, 'but to give you a chariot worth three times seven bondmaids and equipment for twelve men; and a piece of the fine plain of Aí as big as Muirthemne Plain, and a permanent residence in Crúachan, that comes with as much wine as you want; and freedom forever from tax and tribute for you and your kith and kin; and my leaf-shaped brooch of gold that weighs ten score ounces and ten score half-ounces and ten score cross-measures and ten score quarters; and Finnabair, my daughter and Ailill's, as your consort, and the friendship of my own thighs. And if you so require, the gods will guarantee it.'

'Those are great gifts, and great offers!' cried everyone.

'True,' said Fer Diad, 'they are great; but great and all as they are, Medb, I would rather leave them with you than go out to fight my own foster-brother.'

'Well, men,' said Medb, turning away from Fer Diad, for she knew well how to stir things up, 'what Cú Chulainn says is true.'

'What did he say, Medb?' said Fer Diad.

'He said, my dear, that in his province your downfall would be counted as one of his lesser triumphs.'

'It wasn't right of him to say that, for he never found me slow to take up a challenge night or day. I swear by the gods of my people I'll be the first man at the ford of combat tomorrow morning.'

'Bless you! And may you win the fight!' said Medb. 'Now isn't that better than to be thought a coward? Every man feels for his own people. And if it is right for him to stand up for Ulster, just because his mother came from Ulster, why shouldn't you stand up for Connacht, and you the son of a Connacht king?'

So the deal was done, and they made these verses:

Medb:

> A power of rings I give,
> extensive woods and plain,
> freedom for all your kin,
>      as long as they live.
> Ah, Fer Diad Mac Damáin,
> you shall watch your wealth grow.
> Accept what is given –
>      others have done so.

Fer Diad:

> Not without guarantee.
> Though I'm not without skill,
> hard is tomorrow's deed –
>      the man's hard to kill.
> Hound is his proper name,
> difficult to put down.
> He is no easy game,
>      he's hard to turn round.

Medb:

> There's no need to be shy.
> You can choose whom you please
> from high kings and princes
> as firm guarantees.
>      They are honourable men
> and as much as your due,
> for you'll kill the man
>      when the man comes to you.

Fer Diad:

> I'll not give what you ask
> without six men at least.
> When I take on the task
>      the army will watch.

So give me what I ask
and I'll go out to win
though I may be no match
        for hard Cú Chulainn.

Medb:


Take solid men or thieves,
take one of the wordsmiths
as your sure guarantees
        and sure witnesses.
And you can have Morand
and Coirpre Mac Manand
and two of our own sons
        if you so demand.

Fer Diad:


O Medb of the high boast
whom no king can confound,
there's no doubt who is best
        to rule Crúachan's mound.
By your words brave and bold
give me the speckled silk
and the silver and gold
        at your own sweet will.
Give me these as my guard
and I'll give you my hand
that I'll chant his requiem
        though he be so hard.

Medb:


O soldier of soldiers,
take this round brooch in lieu,
and rest until Sunday,
        when the fight is due.
O hero of heroes,
every jewel on earth

shall be given to you –
it's no less than your worth.
And you shall have Finnabair,
the queen of the west,
when the Forge-Hound is killed,
and you come out best.

The great Ulster warrior, Fergus Mac Róich, was present while the deal was being done. He went back to his tent.

'I'm sickened by the deed that will be done tomorrow morning,' he said.

'What deed?' said the people in his tent.

'The killing of my good foster-son, Cú Chulainn.'

'Never! Who dares?'

'Easily told: his own dearly beloved foster-brother, Fer Diad Mac Damáin. Will one of you, out of fellow-feeling for him, go and give him my blessing,' said Fergus, 'and warn him not to be at the ford tomorrow?'

'By the gods,' they said, 'if you yourself were at the ford of battle, we wouldn't go on such a mission.'

'Well, driver,' said Fergus, 'get the horses and hitch up the chariot.'

The charioteer went and got the horses and hitched up the chariot.

They set out for the ford of battle, where Cú Chulainn was stationed.

'A single chariot approaches, Little Hound,' said Láeg.

'What kind of chariot?' said Cú Chulainn.

'A chariot built on royal lines, with a solid gold yoke, a great copper panel, bronze shafts and an armoured canopy, sleek and slender-bodied, straight as an arrow, drawn by two spirited, eager, wild and willing black horses. Poised in the chariot is a kingly warrior with a commanding gaze and a great, flowing, forked, waist-length beard that could shelter fifty comrades on a day of storm and rain. He carries a great glowing cauldron of a shield, beautifully crafted, with three concentric circles and a circumference so broad that its ox-hide covering would make a litter-bed for four squads of ten men. He has a long, keen-edged, mighty broadsword in a scabbard inlaid with silver filigree. Beside him in the chariot, a powerful, triple-bladed, silver-banded spear.'

'Not hard to recognize,' said Cú Chulainn. 'It's my comrade Fergus, moved by fellow-feeling to come and warn me against the four provinces of Ireland.'

Fergus came up to them and dismounted from his chariot.

'Well met, comrade Fergus,' said Cú Chulainn.

'A trusty welcome,' said Fergus.

'Trusty indeed,' said Cú Chulainn. 'If a flock of wildfowl landed on the plain, I'd give you a goose and share another; if fishes crowded the river-mouths, I'd give you a salmon and share another, with a fistful of watercress or marshwort or samphire, and a drink of cold water from the sand to wash it all down.'

'That's a meal fit for an outlaw,' said Fergus.

'Too true. The outlaw's lot has been mine,' said Cú Chulainn, 'from the Monday after Samhain, for since then no one has entertained me as a guest for one night, but I have been standing as a bulwark against the men of Ireland.'

'Had I come with entertainment,' said Fergus, 'I'd be the better pleased for it, but that's not why I came.'

'So why did you come?' said Cú Chulainn.

'To tell you of the warrior who'll go out to meet you and come against you and do combat with you tomorrow morning,' said Fergus.

'Let me know, then. Let me hear it from you,' said Cú Chulainn.

'Your own foster-brother, Fer Diad Mac Damáin.'

'I swear he's the last person I would like to come up against,' said Cú Chulainn, 'not because I fear him, but because of my great love for him.'

'You should fear him, all the same,' said Fergus, 'for when he fights he wears a skin of horn. No weapon nor blade can pierce it.'

'That's neither here nor there,' said Cú Chulainn, 'for I swear by the solemn oath of my people that his every limb and joint will bend before my sword the way a reed is bent in a stream, once he comes across me in the ford.'

So they spoke, and made these verses:

Fergus:

> Cú Chulainn, you are well met.
> It's time for you to engage
> with Fer Diad, who comes for you
> sped by anger, red with rage.

Cú Chulainn:

> Here I stand, no flimsy sail
> against the men of Ireland,
> never to retreat, nor fail
> to take on an opponent.

Fergus:

> For all your fame, Cú Chulainn,
> Fer Diad is not to be scorned.
> He too is renowned in war.
> No blade can pierce his skin of horn.

Cú Chulainn:

> When noble Fer Diad and I
> come together at the ford,
> there will be no holding back
> as we clash sword against sword.

Fergus:

> Empowered by his red sword,
> he matches courage with rage.
> He is safe a hundredfold
> from every point and edge.

Cú Chulainn:

> Hush, Fergus. No more of this,
> powerful though your weapons be.
> In whatever ford I fight,
> no odds can overwhelm me.

Fergus:

> Cú Chulainn of the red sword,
> my heart would fill with delight
> if you carried off the spoils
> from Fer Diad in all his pride.

Cú Chulainn:

> I'm not given to vain boasts,
> and I swear I'll be the one
> to take the victory over
> Dáman Mac Dáire's son.

Fergus:

> When I turned my face back east
> heroes left their homes for me.
> I led armies from the west –
> Ulster's price for wronging me.

Cú Chulainn:

> You'd have found it harder still
> if Conchobar were on his feet.
> Then Medb's ill-begotten march
> would be difficult indeed.

Fergus:

> A greater deed is at hand.
> Arm yourself well, Cú Chulainn
> with the barbed spear. Aim it hard
> against Fer Diad Mac Damáin.

Then Cú Chulainn said:

'Is this all you came to tell me, comrade Fergus?'

'That's the gist of it,' said Fergus.

'It's lucky,' said Cú Chulainn, 'that no one else came to me with such a gist, unless he brought the whole Irish army with him, for I don't think much of being warned against a single warrior.'

Then Fergus went back to his tent.

As for Cú Chulainn:

'What have you planned for tonight?' said Láeg.

'What do you mean?' said Cú Chulainn.

'When Fer Diad comes looking for you, he'll be freshly beautified, washed and bathed, his hair nicely trimmed and plaited, and the four provinces of Ireland will assemble to watch the contest. It seems to me you should go where you'll get the same treatment, to Emer of the Beautiful Hair, who's waiting for you in Two Oxen Meadow at Cairthenn near Sliab Fúait.'

So Cú Chulainn went and spent the night with his wife. As to what happened there, it is not discussed here.

Meanwhile Fer Diad went to his tent. He let his followers know that he had made a contract with Medb to meet Cú Chulainn in single combat the next day, or else to fight six warriors; and by the same token, if he killed Cú Chulainn, to have the same six brought in to ensure that she fulfilled her promises to him.

The atmosphere was gloomy in the tent that night. His supporters felt certain that when those supreme pillars of battle met, there would be a double downfall, or that the only fall would be that of their lord. For it was no easy task to take on Cú Chulainn on the Táin.

Great anxieties troubled Fer Diad that night, and kept him from sleeping. For one thing, if he didn't go and fight this one man, he would lose the bounty and the girl. Moreover, he would have to take on the six warriors, as according to the contract. But most of all he feared that once he appeared before Cú Chulainn at the ford, he could never again call his body and soul his own.

Fer Diad was up early the next morning.

'Well, my friend,' he said, 'get the horses and hitch up the chariot.'

'Upon my word,' said the charioteer, 'I don't know which is worse, to go on this mission or not to go at all.'

Fer Diad talked to his charioteer to give him courage, and they made this song:

Fer Diad:

> Let us go to the fight,
> let us take arms and seek
> the man down at the ford
>     where the Badb will shriek.
> Let's take on Cú Chulainn
> and I'll pierce his thin frame
> with the point of my spear.
>     His death is my aim.

Charioteer:

> For all of your fine talk,
> it's better to stay here.
> One man will not come back –
>     that parting is clear.
> No good will come of it.
> Before all of Ulster
> you will make history –
>     a great disaster.

Fer Diad:

> Your words are out of place.
> To be timid and weak
> is not warrior's work.
>     And I'll not hold back.

> So give over, my friend,
> exchange meekness for might,
> take your life in your hands.
> Now let's go and fight.

The charioteer got the horses and hitched them up to the chariot and they drove out of the camp.

'Hold on,' said Fer Diad. 'It's not right to leave without first bidding farewell to the men of Ireland. Turn the horses and the chariot towards them.'

The charioteer turned the horses and the chariot three times and faced the men of Ireland.

Medb happened to be passing water on the floor of her tent.

'Is Ailill still asleep?' said Medb.

'Not at all,' said Ailill.

'Do you not hear your new son-in-law bidding you farewell?'

'Is that what he's doing?' said Ailill.

'He is indeed,' said Medb, 'for I swear by the oath of my people that the same man who's bidding you farewell will not be coming back to you on his own two feet.'

'Still, we'll have done well out of the match,' said Ailill, 'if he kills Cú Chulainn. It's no odds to us if both of them die. Though we might prefer it if Fer Diad escaped.'

Fer Diad went on to the ford of combat.

'Look and see if Cú Chulainn is at the ford,' said Fer Diad to his charioteer.

'He's not there,' said the charioteer.

'Then take a closer look,' said Fer Diad.

'He's no tiny mite in hiding, wherever he is,' said the charioteer.

'True, my friend. But until today Cú Chulainn never thought a real warrior would come to meet him on the Táin Bó Cúailnge, and when he heard of one, he quit the ford.'

'It's a shame you have to bad-mouth Cú Chulainn behind

his back,' said the charioteer. 'Do you not remember the time when both of you came up against Germán Garbglas the Grey Wolf, above the shores of the Tyrrhene sea, and the enemy got your sword, and Cú Chulainn killed a hundred warriors to get it back, and how he gave the sword into your hands? And do you remember where we stayed that night?'

'I do not,' said Fer Diad.

'At Scáthach's steward's place,' said the charioteer, 'and you were the first one to march blithely in before us, and the steward, blackguard that he was, got you in the small of your back with his three-pronged butcher's meat-hook, and pitched you out the door. Cú Chulainn went in after us and swung his sword at the brute and cut him in two. Then I was your steward for the duration. And if only for that one day, you can't say that you're a better warrior than Cú Chulainn.'

'You would have done better, my friend,' said Fer Diad, 'to remind me of this before, and then I wouldn't have come looking for this fight. Why don't you pull up the shafts of the chariot beside me and put the leather covering under my head, and let me sleep a while?'

'You'd be as well,' said the charioteer, 'to sleep in the path of a stag hunt!'

'What's the matter, my friend? Can you not keep watch for me?'

'I'll watch for you surely,' said the charioteer, 'and unless they come for you out of the clouds or thin air, I'll see them coming, east or west, and give you fair warning.'

The chariot-shafts were pulled up beside him, and the leather covering put under his head, but not a wink did he sleep.

As for Cú Chulainn, he didn't get up until the sun was well risen in the sky, for he didn't want the men of Ireland to think that fear had driven him to an early start.

'Now, comrade Láeg, get the horses and hitch up the chariot. Fer Diad will be up early, and waiting for us.'

The charioteer got the horses and hitched them up. Cú

Chulainn got into the chariot and they drove out for the ford.

Fer Diad's charioteer wasn't long watching when he heard the rumble of the chariot coming towards them. He alerted his master, and made this song:

> I hear chariot-noise.
> I see its silver yoke,
> a huge human form poised
>     above the hard prow,
> creak of the axle-tree
> through the heroic wood
> as it approaches us
>     in its amplitude –
>
> a deft Hound at the helm,
> who urges his horses
> with hawk-like vigilance
>     right into our realm.
> Surely these are his steeds
> that loom from the red mist
> as their master brings us
>     disaster indeed.
>
> I foresaw this last year:
> a man waits by the mound
> at his appointed hour
>     to meet the Forge-Hound –
> Hound of Emain Macha,
> Hound of the sword and spear,
> ever-changing Shape-Hound.
>     I hear him, and he hears.

'Get up, my friend,' said Fer Diad. 'Get the weapons ready to meet him at the ford.'

'I think if I turned round, the shafts of his chariot would pierce the back of my neck.'

'My friend,' said Fer Diad, 'you sing his praises too highly.
It's not as if he paid you for the poetry.'

And he chanted:

> I need you to help me,
> not to stand by and fret.
> Enough of your praises,
>     for he's no great threat.
> Let Cúailnge's great warrior
> use his every device.
> We have made a bargain –
>     his death is the price.

Charioteer:

> When Cúailnge's great warrior
> arrives in all his might
> he'll drive at us head-on,
>     not from us in flight.
> Give praise where praise is due.
> He strikes the battle-road
> like water off a cliff –
>     or a thunderbolt.

Fer Diad:

> So much have you praised him,
> we might yet come to blows.
> You've stood in awe of him
>     since we left home.
> All those who challenge him
> praise this man to the sky.
> They go out to meet him –
>     and then the fools die.

Not long afterwards, Cú Chulainn arrived at the ford. Fer
Diad stood on the south side, Cú Chulainn on the north side.
Fer Diad bade Cú Chulainn welcome.

'Well met, Cú Chulainn,' said Fer Diad.

'There was a time when I could have trusted that welcome,' said Cú Chulainn, 'but now I can trust it no more. And Fer Diad,' he said, 'by rights I should have done the welcoming, and not you, for you have entered my territory. And by rights you should not challenge me, but I should challenge you, for you have driven off our women, our young fellows and our boys, our steeds and our horses, and our herds and droves of cattle.'

'Oh, very good, Cú Chulainn,' said Fer Diad, 'and what makes you think you're fit for this contest? When we were with Scáthach and Uathach and Aífe, you were my lackey, the boy who looked after my spears and made up my bed.'

'That's true,' said Cú Chulainn. 'I did so then because I was young and small, but things are not so now, for there isn't a warrior in the world that I couldn't repel.'

Then each reproached the other bitterly as they renounced their friendship. And Fer Diad made a verse, and Cú Chulainn replied:

Fer Diad:

What brings you, little Cú,
to take on a real man?
Your flesh will drip red through
    the steam of your horses.
Your journey's in vain,
for one stick makes no fire.
You'll be cold when they bring you
    home to your byre.

Cú Chulainn:

I come like a wild boar
to overthrow the rule
of armies. I'll drive them
    into a dark pool.

Red rage empowers me
to wreak havoc and strife
on the bargaining pawn
    that you call your life.

Fer Diad:

It is I who will crush.
It is I who will kill,
for you'll buckle under
    the force of my will.
Before all of Ulster,
and before tomorrow,
you will be history –
    a great disaster.

Cú Chulainn:

Is this how we should fight,
exchanging bitter words
like two groaning corpses?
    Let's plunge into the ford
with our life in our hands
before the gaping hordes
to find death by keen spear
    and bloodthirsty sword.

Fer Diad:

Let us do what we must
before sunset tonight.
This battle at Boirche
    will prove I can fight.
I'll horrify Ulster.
I'll make a bloody ghost
of you, accompanied by
    the groans of the host.

Cú Chulainn:

> You've walked into the gap.
> You're in the danger zone.
> Sharp weapons will pierce you
> and cleave flesh and bone.
> This hero will take you
> to another place
> where you will find nothing
> but death and disgrace.

Fer Diad:

> Your threats are worth nothing.
> Your boasting comes to this:
> when you ask for quarter,
> I'll be merciless.
> For I know you of old,
> bird-hearted little boy –
> when it comes to the bit,
> you're not very bold.

Cú Chulainn:

> When we stayed with Scáthach
> we were never apart
> in courage or in war.
> We shared the same heart.
> You were my best comrade.
> We breathed the same air.
> You were dear above all.
> I'll miss you, I swear.

Fer Diad:

> You shrink before the fight.
> All your honour is fled,
> and before the cock crows
> I'll have spiked your head.

> Cú Chulainn of Cúailnge,
> your wits are atilt,
> and you'll be sorry for it,
>      for yours is the guilt.

'Not so, Fer Diad,' said Cú Chulainn, 'for you did wrong to come and fight me. You were lured by Ailill and Medb's low cunning. As for all those others who were lured to fight me, they got no gain or profit from it, for they all died at my hands. And you will get no gain or profit by it, and you will die at my hands.'

And having said that, he went on to say:

> Come no closer, Fer Diad,
> for you'll come off worse than me.
> Comrade, step back, or you'll bring
> sorrow to your company.

> Come no closer to the wrong;
> this way takes you to your grave.
> Why should you alone escape
> my unconquerable rage?

> I'll overwhelm you with skill,
> horn-skinned man, tough as you are.
> And that girl you boast about
> will be that one step too far.

> That Medb's daughter Finnabair
> for all her seeming treasure
> and the fairness of her form
> will never give you pleasure.

> Finnabair the king's daughter,
> as the matter is revealed,
> led men into her sweet snare
> and their fate, and yours, was sealed.

O break not your word to me,
that straight word of man to man,
our promises and pledges:
come no closer though you can.

This is the girl who was sworn
to fifty soldiers. My spear
found theirs wanting. I pierced them
through and through. They died in fear.

Fer Báeth was a fierce warrior,
a hero among heroes.
Yet I soon put out his fire.
I snuffed him out with one blow.

Subdaire found a bitter end.
A hundred women loved him –
a well-dressed man, with rich friends.
And not one of them saved him.

If they'd offered her to me,
and she had offered me her breast,
I would not wound yours – no, not
north nor south nor east nor west.

'So, Fer Diad,' said Cú Chulainn, 'that's why you shouldn't
come to fight me. For when we were with Scáthach and
Uathach and Aífe, we used to go together into battle and the
fields of contest, every fight and every combat, into the forests
and the wastelands and every dark and secret place.'
And having said that, he said this:

Two hearts that beat as one,
we were comrades in the woods,
men who shared a bed
and the same deep sleep

after heavy fighting
in strange territories.
Apprentices of Scáthach,
we would ride out together
to explore the dark woods.

Fer Diad said:

Cú Chulainn, you have deft skills,
but I have mastered them as well.
Foul play has separated us
and paid for your first defeat.
Forget our brotherhood.
You'll gain nothing by it.

'We've talked too much,' said Fer Diad. 'What weapons shall we use today, Cú Chulainn?'

'It's your choice of weapons until nightfall,' said Cú Chulainn, 'for you were first to the ford.'

'Do you remember,' said Fer Diad, 'the martial arts we practised under Scáthach and Uathach and Aífe?'

'I remember them well,' said Cú Chulainn.

'Then if you remember, let's do it.'

So they began with those martial arts. They took up their two special shields, and their eight sharp throwing-discs, and their eight darts, and their eight long, bone-hilted knives and their eight smaller bone-hilted darts that flew between them like bees in fine weather. Every throw was true. They hurled the weapons at each other from the half-light of early morning until high noon, all the while fending them off with the knobs and bosses of the special shields. No matter how good the throw, their defence was equal to it, and neither of them drew blood from the other during all that time.

'Let's lay off these weapons,' said Fer Diad. 'We'll reach no conclusion this way.'

'Very well,' said Cú Chulainn, 'if it's time to lay off, let's lay off.'

They laid off then and threw the weapons to their charioteers.

'What weapons shall we use now, Cú Chulainn?' said Fer Diad.

'It's still your choice of weapons until nightfall,' said Cú Chulainn, 'since you were first to the ford.'

'Then,' said Fer Diad, 'let's try our smooth, sharp, hard, slender spears bound with flax cord.'

'Very well,' said Cú Chulainn, 'let's do that.'

They took up their two equally hard, strong shields, and their smooth, sharp, hard, slender spears bound with flax cord. They threw their spears at each other from noon till evening. Good as their defence was, their throwing was better still, and they wounded and bloodied each other for that length of time.

'Let's lay off these weapons,' said Fer Diad. 'We'll reach no conclusion this way.'

'Very well,' said Cú Chulainn, 'if it's time to lay off, let's lay off.'

They laid off then and threw the weapons to their charioteers.

Then they came up to each other and each put an arm around the other's shoulders, and gave him three kisses. Their horses grazed together that night and their charioteers warmed themselves by the same fire. And their charioteers made beds and pillows of fresh rushes for the wounded men. Then teams of doctors came to salve them and heal them, and they put soothing plants and herbs and curing charms to their countless cuts and stabs and gashes. For every soothing plant and herb and curing charm that was put to the countless cuts and stabs and gashes of Cú Chulainn, he sent the same to Fer Diad on the south side of the ford, so that the men of Ireland could not say, if Fer Diad fell by his hand, that it was because he got better care. And for every piece of food and pleasant, wholesome and reviving drink that the men of Ireland gave Fer Diad, he sent the same to Cú Chulainn on the north side of the ford; Fer Diad had more suppliers than Cú Chulainn, for he was looked after by all the men of Ireland, but only the people of Bregia Plain were looking after Cú Chulainn. They attended to him on a daily basis.

They stayed there that night. They got up early the next morning and went out to the ford of battle.

'What weapons shall we use today, Fer Diad?' said Cú Chulainn.

'It's your choice of weapons until nightfall,' said Fer Diad, 'for it was my choice yesterday.'

'Then,' said Cú Chulainn, 'let's try our beloved broad stabbing-spears, for we might get closer to the final blow today by stabbing than by yesterday's throwing. And let the horses be brought out and hitched up to the chariots. Today we'll fight from chariot and horse.'

'Let's do that,' said Fer Diad.

So that day they took up their specially strengthened broad-shields and their beloved broad stabbing-spears, and began to stab and cut each other, pushing and thrusting from the half-light of early morning until the evening sunset. If it were customary for birds in flight to pass through men's bodies, they would have flown through their bodies that day and brought with them gobbets of blood and flesh through their open cuts into the air and the clouds beyond. By evening the horses were done and the charioteers dead beat and the great heroes themselves were ready to drop.

'Let's lay off now, Fer Diad,' said Cú Chulainn, 'for our horses are done and our charioteers dead beat, and if they're crying out for rest, why shouldn't we cry out for rest too?'

And having said that, he said:

No more juddering of wheels
or Titan-struggle.
Let the noise of battle cease.
Tie up the horses.

'Very well,' said Fer Diad, 'if it's time to lay off, let's lay off.'

They laid off then and threw their weapons to their charioteers. Then they came up to each other and each put an arm around the other's shoulders, and gave him three kisses. Their horses grazed together that night and their charioteers warmed themselves by the same fire. And their charioteers made beds and pillows of fresh rushes for the wounded men. Then teams of doctors came to examine them and watch over them and tend them that night. So terrible were their countless cuts and stabs and gashes that all that could be done was to lay amulets on them and chant spells over them to staunch the flow of blood and ease the pain. For every amulet and spell and charm that was laid on Cú Chulainn's cuts and gashes, he sent the same to Fer Diad on the south side of the ford. And for every piece of food, and pleasant, wholesome and reviving drink that the men of Ireland gave Fer Diad, he sent the same to Cú Chulainn on the north side of the ford; Fer Diad had more suppliers than Cú Chulainn, for he was looked after by all the men of Ireland, but only the people of Brega Plain were looking after Cú Chulainn. They came to visit him and talk to him on a daily basis.

They stayed there that night. They got up early the next morning and proceeded to the ford of battle. That day Cú Chulainn noted Fer Diad's haggard and ghastly appearance.

'You do not look well today, Fer Diad,' he said. 'Your hair has grown dull overnight, and your eye is clouded. You are not in good shape.'

'It's not from any fear or dread of you,' said Fer Diad, 'for there's not a warrior in Ireland I can't overcome.'

Cú Chulainn lamented and pitied him then. With Fer Diad
making answer, he spoke these words:

> Fer Diad, if this be you,
> now I know it was your fate
> when a woman sent you here
> to fight against your comrade.

Fer Diad:

> Cú Chulainn, you know what's known
> by any soldier brave:
> every man must step upon
> the sod that is his grave.

Cú Chulainn:

> Medb's daughter Finnabair
> with whom you pleasured your sight
> was not given out of love
> but for you to prove your might.

Fer Diad:

> My might is long since proven,
> O meticulous Hound;
> and until this very day
> no one braver has been found.

Cú Chulainn:

> Son of Dáman Mac Dáire,
> you have played the renegade –
> coming at a woman's word
> to fight against your comrade.

Fer Diad:

> Though we are partners, dear Hound,
> should we part without a fight
> my good name and renown
> would be shamed by Ailill and Medb.

Cú Chulainn:

> Food has not passed his lips,
> nor was the man ever born
> to high king or shining queen
> for whose sake I'd do you harm.

Fer Diad:

> Cú Chulainn, I know well
> that Medb betrayed us to the hilt.
> You will win victory and fame
> and do so free of all guilt.

Cú Chulainn:

> My brave heart is a dead weight,
> my soul near torn from its roots;
> I'd welcome any other fate,
> than to fight you, Fer Diad.

'You can fault me all you like today,' said Fer Diad. 'What weapons shall we use?'

'It's your choice of weapons until nightfall today,' said Cú Chulainn. 'It was my choice yesterday.'

'Then,' said Fer Diad, 'let's try our great broadswords. We might get closer to the final blow today by hacking rather than yesterday's stabbing.'

'Let's do it, then,' said Cú Chulainn.

So they took up their two great full-length shields. They lifted their heavy hacking-swords and began to hack and hew each other, slashing and striking and cutting lumps the size of a baby's head from each other's shoulders and flanks and backs. They hacked away at each other like this from the half-light of early morning until the evening sunset.

'Let's lay off, Cú Chulainn,' said Fer Diad.

'Very well,' said Cú Chulainn, 'if it's time to lay off, let's lay off.'

So they laid off and threw their weapons to their charioteers.

And they were two sad men who parted that night, so sorrow-
ful and sick at heart that it seemed the pair who had met that
morning were happy men, radiating joy and walking on air.
Their horses did not graze together that night, nor did their
charioteers warm themselves by the same fire.

They spent the night there. Fer Diad got up early the next
morning and went alone to the ford of battle, for he knew
that this would be the decisive day of their encounter, and
that one or other, or both, would fall. He put on his battle-
garb before he went to meet Cú Chulainn. This was the outfit:
next to his fair skin, the apron of filmy silk with a variegated
gold border; over that, the apron of stitched brown leather;
over that, a sheet of rock the size of a millstone; and over
that, for fear and dread of the *gae bolga*, he put on a double-
thick apron of double-smelted iron. He set on his head the
battle-hardened war-helmet elaborately decorated with forty
precious carbuncles, and studded with tesserae of red enamel
and crystal and rubies and gleaming gems from the East. In
his right hand he took his deadly, death-dealing spear. In his
left he took his curved battle-sword with the gold pommel
and hilt of red gold. On the arch-slope of his back he slung
his massive horn shield with its fifty knobs and bosses, each
big enough to cup a prize boar, not to speak of the great
central boss of red gold. That day Fer Diad displayed many
amazing and manifold feats that he had learned from no
one – not foster-mother nor foster-father, nor Scáthach nor
Uathach nor Aífe – but were inspired that day by the prospect
of coming up against Cú Chulainn.

Cú Chulainn arrived at the ford and saw Fer Diad's many
amazing and manifold feats.

'Observe, comrade Láeg, the many amazing and manifold
feats displayed by Fer Diad, for he will deploy them against
me when the time comes. And if at any time my defeat seems
imminent, you must needle and nettle me and bad-mouth
me to get my temper up. But if at any time his defeat seems

imminent, you must applaud me and sing my praises and cheer me on to even greater efforts.'

'You can count on me, little Cú,' said Láeg.

Then Cú Chulainn put on his war-hardened battle-garb and displayed many amazing and manifold feats he had learned from no one, not Scáthach nor Uathach nor Aífe. Fer Diad observed those feats and knew they would be deployed against him when the time came.

'How shall we fight today, Fer Diad?' said Cú Chulainn.

'It's your choice how we'll fight until nightfall,' said Fer Diad.

'Then,' said Cú Chulainn, 'let's try ford-combat.'

'By all means let us try that,' said Fer Diad.

Even as he said it, he knew that ford-combat was the last thing he wanted to undertake, for no warrior or great soldier had ever overcome Cú Chulainn in ford-combat. Great deeds were done by the two heroes that day in the ford, by those two champion fighters of Western Europe, those two bright torches of Irish bravery, those two most liberal and lavish givers of gifts and trophies in the north-west of the world, those two keys to Ireland's feats of arms, brought head to head by the low trickery of Ailill and Medb. They brought all their skills to bear on one another from the half-light of early morning until high noon, and when noon came the rage of the two men mounted to fever pitch as they bore closer and closer to each other.

Then Cú Chulainn made a leap from the brink of the ford on to the great central boss of Fer Diad Mac Damáin's shield to strike down at his head from over the rim of the shield. Fer Diad gave the shield a dunt with his left elbow and threw Cú Chulainn off like a bird on to the brink of the ford. Again Cú Chulainn made a leap from the brink of the ford on to the great central boss of Fer Diad's shield to strike down at his head over the rim of the shield. Fer Diad gave the shield a dunt with his left knee and threw Cú Chulainn off like a baby on to the brink of the ford.

Láeg saw what was happening.

'Some contest!' he said. 'The enemy cuffs you as a mother cuffs a bad child! He beats you up like flax in a pond! He grinds you like malt in a mill! He goes through you like a drill through oak! He climbs all over you like ivy over a tree! He's a hawk, and you're a sparrow! And never again can you call yourself a proper warrior, or boast about your great deeds and skill at arms, you twisted little imp!'

Cú Chulainn rose up for the third time, quick as the wind and swift as a swallow, dragon-like and angry as a storm, and landed on the great central boss of Fer Diad's shield to strike down at his head over the rim of the shield. The warrior gave a shake of the shield that hurled Cú Chulainn off into the middle of the ford as if he hadn't been there in the first place.

With that Cú Chulainn torqued himself a hundredfold. He swelled and bellied like a bladder full of breath until he arched up over Fer Diad like a monstrously distorted rainbow, tall and horrible as a Fomorian giant[2] or a deep-sea merman.

Then so closely did they fight each other that they grappled head to head and foot to foot and hand to hand beyond the shelter of their shields, which burst and split from boss to rim, so closely did they fight. So closely did they fight, their spear-points bent and buckled from tip to rivet. So closely did they fight that the ear-splitting shrill-shrieking of their swords and shields and spears as their edges clashed was echoed by the shrieks and screeches of the goblins and ghouls and sprites of the glens and the fiends of the air. So closely did they fight that the river was tossed from its course and its bed and left room enough for the final resting-chamber of a great king or queen, with not a drip nor drop in it save what was splashed up by the two champions as they trampled and scattered the mud of the floor of the ford. So closely did they fight that the horses of the Irish army reared up and went buck-mad and broke loose from their ropes and reins and shackles and the women and children and youngsters and cripples and madmen broke out south-westward from the camp.

They were deep into sword-fighting when Cú Chulainn let his guard drop and in that instant Fer Diad sank his ivory-hilted blade into Cú Chulainn's breast and the blood spouted over his belt to run red into the ford from the warrior's body. Cú Chulainn could no longer endure Fer Diad's overwhelming onslaught of cut and thrust and he called out to Láeg for the *gae bolga*. This was what the *gae bolga* was: it was cast downstream for him, and was thrown from the fork of the foot; it made a single wound when it entered a man's body, whereupon it opened up into thirty barbs, and it could not be taken from a man's body without the flesh being cut away from around it.

When Fer Diad heard the *gae bolga* being called for he dropped his shield to cover the lower parts of his body. Cú Chulainn launched a javelin from the cup of his hand over the rim of Fer Diad's shield to bypass the edge of his horn-skin so that it drove through the heart in his breast and out from his back to the half of its length. Fer Diad pulled up his shield to cover the upper parts of his body, but that was help that came too late.

'Here comes the *gae bolga*,' said the charioteer, and he sent it downstream.

Cú Chulainn caught it in the fork of his foot and launched it at Fer Diad and it went through the double-thick apron of double-smelted iron and broke in three the sheet of rock the size of a millstone and entered the rear portal of Fer Diad's body to fill every nook and cranny of him with its barbs.

'That's enough for now,' said Fer Diad. 'That's done for me. And it was a powerful throw from your right foot. It wouldn't be right to die by your hand.'

He uttered these words:

> Hound of the great deeds,
> you killed me wrongly.
> Your guilt bleeds on me
> as my blood stains you.

The gap of deceit
is where men find death.
I struggle for words.
I draw my last breath.

My ribs are all crushed,
my heart thick with blood.
I have not fought well.
Hound, I am done for.

Cú Chulainn went to him and put his two arms around
him and carried him, armour, weapons and all, north across
the ford so that all that remained of Fer Diad would be on
the north side of the ford and not on the south side with the
men of Ireland. Cú Chulainn set Fer Diad down there and as
he did so he was smitten by a sudden daze of faintness and
fell to the ground. Láeg saw this and feared the men of Ireland
might then attack him.

'Get up, little Cú!' said Láeg. 'The men of Ireland will come
to attack us and they won't be interested in single combat,
now that you have killed Fer Diad Mac Damáin.'

'Why should I get up, my friend,' he said, 'and this one
fallen by my hand?'

Then, with Cú Chulainn answering, the charioteer spoke
these words:

On your feet, great battle-hound!
Bring all your courage to bear!
You felled Fer Diad of the hosts,
though the fight was hard, I swear!

Cú Chulainn:

What use have I for courage?
I am driven mad with pain
for my great deed – this body
I pierced again and again.

*Láeg:*

> There's no need to grieve for him.
> Indeed you should boast instead.
> He too stuck his spear in you
> and left you wounded half-dead.

Cú Chulainn:

> He could have cut off my arm,
> my leg, and still I would mourn
> Fer Diad of the steeds, who was
> part of me, and breathes no more.

Láeg:

> The daughters of the Red Branch[3]
> are not sorry, that's for sure.
> Fer Diad dead and you alive –
> that parting they can endure.

Cú Chulainn:

> Since the day I left Cúailnge
> to watch for Connacht's great queen,
> the number of her hordes I killed
> she holds in grave esteem.

Láeg:

> Watching over your own herds
> you have not slept in peace,
> waking early most mornings
> when your company was least.

Then Cú Chulainn began to grieve and lament for Fer Diad, and spoke these words:

'Ah, Fer Diad, it was a sorry thing that you didn't speak with those who knew my high, brave deeds, before you came to fight me.

'A sorry thing, that Láeg Mac Riangabra did not put you to shame with stories of our fostering together.

'A sorry thing, that you turned away from Fergus's sound advice.

'A sorry thing, that Conall, kind and brave, experienced in battle, could not have helped your sorry case.

'For these are men who do not heed the whims and whisperings and false promises of fair-headed Connachtwomen. These are men who could have told you that there will not be born among the Connachtmen a being to achieve the overwhelming greatness of my deeds with sword and javelin and shield, with chess and draughts and horse and chariot.

'And never will there be a hero's hand to hack the flesh of warriors like the honourable hand of Fer Diad. The redmouthed Badb will never screech again so loud above the shields that glimmer in the gap of battle. And never till the day of doom will Crúachan get the bargain that they got in you, O bright-faced son of Damán.'

Then Cú Chulainn got up and stood over Fer Diad.

'Ah, Fer Diad,' said Cú Chulainn, 'greatly did the men of Ireland deceive you and abandon you when they sent you to oppose and fight me, for to oppose and fight me on the Táin Bó Cúailnge is no easy task.'

And having said that, he spoke these words:

> Ah, Fer Diad, you were betrayed.
> Our last meeting led to this,
> my everlasting sorrow
> that I live while you are dead.
>
> When, overseas with Scáthach
> we learned victory, we thought then
> our friendship would last until
> time itself came to an end.

I loved the blush in your cheek,
your fine, upstanding young form,
your clear eye, your way of speech.
I loved the way you held yourself.

No one ever tore into
a fight with such fierce attack
nor bore shield on his broad back
like you, Damán's bright-faced son.

Never till this very day,
since I slew Aífe's one son
have I met in fight or fray
one as powerful as you.

And Medb's daughter Finnabair,
that beautiful bait you hoped
would be yours? You might as well
try to tie sand with a rope.

Cú Chulainn was gazing at Fer Diad.

'Well, comrade Láeg,' said Cú Chulainn, 'you can strip Fer Diad now. Take off his battle-gear and garments, and let me see the brooch he entered battle for.'

Láeg came forward and stripped Fer Diad. He took off his battle-gear and his garments, and Cú Chulainn saw the brooch, and he began to mourn and lament. He spoke these words:

Ah, dear golden brooch,
bright and victorious
Fer Diad of the hosts,
I mourn your strong arm,

your curled yellow hair
like a golden blaze,
the soft leaf-shaped belt
you wore at your waist.

Our comradeship was
keen as a bright sword.
It was a gleaming shield,
a noble chess-board.

You fell by my hand.
I cannot revoke
that ungentle fight.
Ah, dear golden brooch!

'Now, comrade Láeg,' said Cú Chulainn, 'cut Fer Diad open
and take the *gae bolga* out of him, for I must have my weapon.'

Láeg came forward and cut Fer Diad open and took out
the *gae bolga*. Cú Chulainn saw his weapon bloody and crimson from Fer Diad's body, and spoke these words:

Fer Diad, a sorry sight –
you are red and yet so pale,
I with my weapon unwiped,
and you in your bed of blood.

When we ventured to the East
with Scáthach and Uathach, who
would have thought of such pale lips
or weapons between us two?

Remember how Scathách spoke
her sharp imperious command –
Soldiers! Forward to the fray!
Germán Garbglas is at hand!

Then to you, Fer Diad, I said –
and to Lugaid also,
and to Fer Báeth, ever-reckless –
let's meet Germán head to head.

We climbed the rocks of battle
above the Lake of Envy
and brought out four hundred men
from the Isles of Victory.

When I stood with brave Fer Diad
on Germán's very threshold,
I killed Rinn Mac Níuil,
he killed Rúad Mac Forníuil.

Out on the shore, Fer Báeth killed
Bláth Mac Colbai of the red sword.
Lugaid, quick as a flash, killed
Mugairne from the Tyrrhene Sea.

After we went in, I slew
four times fifty raging men.
Fer Diad killed that wicked crew,
Dam Dreimed and Dam Dílend.

We razed Germán's cunning fort
above the wide, glittering sea
and took Germán himself alive
to Scáthach of the broad shield.

Our foster-mother bound us
with a blood-pact of goodwill
to all the tribes of Ireland.
This is how it was fulfilled.

Sorry, sorry was the day
that brought Fer Diad to my hand.
I served him a drink of blood.
Now he lies here while I stand.

Had you fallen at the hands
of Greek warriors, my life
would not have outlasted yours,
I would have died by your side.

Sad is the thing that became
Scáthach's two brave foster-sons –
I wounded and dripping gore,
your chariot standing empty.

Sad is the thing that became
Scáthach's two brave foster-sons –
I leak blood from every pore
and you lie dead forever.

Sad is the thing that became
Scáthach's two brave foster-sons –
you dead, I bursting with life.
Courage has a brutal core.

'Now, little Cú,' said Láeg, 'let us leave the ford. We have
been here too long.'

'Very well, let us leave it,' said Cú Chulainn. 'But all the
contest and battles I have ever fought seem only play and
sport compared to my struggle against Fer Diad.'

And he spoke these words:

It was all play, all sport
till Fer Diad came to the ford.
We were brought up the same,
with the same rights,
the same good foster-mother –
she of the great name.

It was all play, all sport
till Fer Diad came to the ford –
we had the same skills,
the same fire and force.
Scáthach gave two shields,
one to Fer Diad, one to me.

It was all play, all sport
till Fer Diad came to the ford –
Ah, pillar of gold
I cut down in the ford,
you were the fierce bull
that towered above all!

It was all play, all sport
till Fer Diad came to the ford –
ferocious lion, brave
overwhelming wave!

It was all play, all sport
till Fer Diad came to the ford –
I thought beloved Fer Diad
would live forever after me –
yesterday, a mountain-side,
today, nothing but a shade.

Three multitudes on the Táin
I took on board as my foes –
great men, horses and cattle
slaughtered in their countless droves.

As for Crúachan's grand army,
of those incalculable hordes
between a third and a half
were killed in my savage sport.

Never fought on battle-field,
nor sucked at Banba's[4] breast,
nor voyaged over land or sea,
a prince so regally possessed.

# X
# THE
# MULTIPLE
# WOUNDS
# OF CETHERN

THE IRISH ARMY drew back southwards from Fer Diad's Ford. Cú Chulainn lay there injured until he was found by an advance party consisting of Senoll Uathach the Awful Old Man and the two sons of Ficce. They took him to the streams and rivers of Conaille Muirthemne to cleanse and heal his wounds. It was a custom of the Túatha Dé Danann to place herbs and healing plants in the rivers of Conaille, so that they were speckled with green. These are the names of those healing waters: Sás the Repose and Búan the Steady and Bithslán the Longlife; Finnglas the Clearwater and Gleóir the Brightwater; Tadc the Tough and Talaméd the Silty; Rinn and Birr, the Point and the Peak; Breinide the Bitter; Cellenn the Hidden and Cumang the Narrow; Gaenemain the Sandy; and Dichú and Muach and Miliuc; and Den and Delt; and Dubglaise the Blackwater.

As Cú Chulainn's wounds were being cleansed, the army continued south and set up camp at Imorach Smiromach, the Border of the Bath of Marrow. Mac Roth the messenger was sent north to scout for the men of Ulster, and went as far as Sliab Fúait to see if any were on their trail. He reported back that he had seen only one chariot.

'I saw a chariot crossing the plain from the north,' said Mac Roth, 'shimmering like the mist of May. In the chariot, a silver-haired man. In his hand, a silver spike, with which he goaded both charioteer and horses, as if he feared he'd never get to us alive. A brindled hunting-dog ran before him.'

'Who might that be, Fergus?' said Ailill. 'Conchobar, perhaps, or Celtchar?'

'I think not,' said Fergus. 'More likely it is Cethern, that generous, bloody-minded son of Fintan.'

So it was. Cethern charged into the camp and killed large numbers of men. He himself was badly wounded, and after the fight he came to Cú Chulainn with his guts hanging about his feet. Cú Chulainn expressed concern for his wounds.

'Get me a doctor,' said Cethern to Cú Chulainn.

A bed of fresh rushes and a pillow was made up for him.

'Now, comrade Láeg,' said Cú Chulainn to his charioteer, 'go to the Irish camp and tell their doctors to come and tend to Cethern Mac Fintain. And if they don't, I swear that though they be hidden underground or in a locked room, I'll kill every last one of them by this time tomorrow.'

The doctors did not relish this prospect, for there was no one in the camp Cethern hadn't injured. But they feared that if they didn't go, Cú Chulainn would kill them. So they went. The first doctor came up and examined Cethern.

'You won't last long,' he said.

'Then neither will you,' said Cethern, and he dealt him such a blow with his fist that his brains spurted out from his ears. In the same way he killed fifty doctors. Or maybe it was fifteen. The last one only got a glancing blow, but even that knocked him unconscious. Cú Chulainn saved him afterwards.

'It wasn't a good idea,' said Cú Chulainn to Cethern, 'to kill the doctors. We'll get none of them to come now.'

'It wasn't a good idea for them to tell me the bad news.'

Then the seer Fíngin – Conchobar's personal doctor – was sent for to examine both Cú Chulainn and Cethern. He was informed of their heavy injuries, and before long they saw his chariot approach. Cú Chulainn went up to him.

'Take a look at Cethern for us,' he said, 'but keep well back, for he's killed fifteen of their doctors.'

Fíngin came forward a little and studied Cethern from a distance.

'See this first wound I got?' said Cethern. 'It looks bad.'

'You got it from a proud and headstrong woman,' said Fíngin.

'No doubt you're right,' said Cethern. 'This tall, good-looking woman came at me. She had a fine, long face and a head of yellow hair. There were two gold birds on her shoulders. She wore a dark purple hooded cloak. There were five handfuls of gold on her back. A keen-edged javelin blazed in one hand, and she held an iron sword aloft in her proud fist. She cut a striking figure. She's the one who first wounded me.'

'A sore wound indeed!' said Cú Chulainn. 'That was Medb of Crúachan.'

'And here,' said the doctor, 'we have a slight, half-hearted wound – the wound of a kinsman. It's not fatal.'

'You're right,' said Cethern. 'This soldier came at me. He carried a curved, sharp-scalloped shield, a spear with a hooked point and a ivory-hilted sword. He wore his hair in a triple crest. He had a brown cloak pinned round him with a silver brooch. I gave him just a little wound back.'

'I know him,' said Cú Chulainn. 'That was Fergus Mac Róich's son Illann.'

'And here,' said the doctor, 'we have the onslaught of two warriors.'

'You're right again,' said Cethern. 'A pair of them came at me. They had two long shields with hammered silver grips and silver bosses. They carried silver-banded five-pronged spears. They wore their hair cropped, and they had silver bands around their necks.'

'I know them,' said Cú Chulainn. 'Oll and Oichne, Big Man and Little Sprout, two foster-sons of Ailill and Medb. They never go to battle without being sure of killing someone. They're the ones who wounded you.'

'Then another pair of them came at me,' said Cethern.

'Their equipment gleamed, and they gleamed too, with their striking looks.'

'I know them,' said Cú Chulainn. 'Bun and Mecon, Trunk and Root, of the king's personal guard.'

'And here we have a very serious wound,' said the doctor. 'They angled into your heart, and crossed spears inside you. I can't guarantee to cure this, but I have wide experience of these matters, and I might find a way to save you. This brutal wound,' the doctor went on, 'was caused by the two sons of the Forest King.'

'So it was,' said Cethern. 'Two warriors with silvery hair came at me like two wooden barrels, one bigger than the other. Just like you said, their two spears crossed inside me.'

'I know them,' said Cú Chulainn. 'They serve in Medb's personal guard – Bróen and Láiréne, Raindrop and Cirrus, the two thunder-and-lightning sons of the Forest King.'

'And here,' said the doctor Fíngin, 'is the triple wound of three nephews.'

'You're right,' said Cethern. 'Three men the spit of each other came at me, linked by a bronze chain spiked with barbs and blades.'

'Those were the three scabbards of Banba, followers of Cú Roí Mac Dáiri.'

'And here another three warriors laid into you,' said Fíngin.

'You're right again,' said Cethern. 'Three hard men came at me, looking like champions, each with a silver torque at his neck, and each with a fistful of spears. The three of them stuck me, and I stuck them back.'

'Those were three of the Fighting Men from Iruath,' said Cú Chulainn.

'They gave you a tricky wound,' said the doctor. 'They cut the strings of your heart and it's rolling about inside you like a ball of yarn in an empty bag. How I'll cure that one, I don't know. And here,' said Fíngin, 'three bloody-minded men hacked into you.'

'Just so,' said Cethern. 'Three big fat men came at me,

discussing what they might do to me even before they reached me, they and their three heads of greasy hair.'

'Those were three of Medb's and Ailill's stewards,' said Cú Chulainn, 'Scenb, Rann and Fodail – Knife, Carve and Serve.'

'And here,' said Fíngin, 'we have three sly blows.'

'Sly indeed,' said Cethern. 'Three so-called warriors crept up on me. They wore tabby shirts and big black shaggy cloaks with bald patches in them. Each wielded an iron club.'

'Those were the Three Rough Men of Baíscne,' said Cú Chulainn, 'skivvies at Medb's table.'

'And here,' said Fíngin, 'two men of the same name dug into you.'

'They did indeed,' said Cethern. 'Two big men in matching dark green cloaks came at me with sharp, curved, scalloped shields and long, green, trowel-headed spears.'

'I know them,' said Cú Chulainn. 'Those were Cormac Colomon ind Ríg, the King's Column, and Cormac Maíle Ogath, the Bald Young Blade.'

'The wounds they made are right close together,' said the doctor. 'They both went for your gullet, and scraped their spears together inside you. And here,' he went on, 'two brothers attacked you.'

'I should think so,' said Cethern. 'I was set on by a pair of curly-headed warriors, one fair, the other dark. Each had a dazzling shield with golden animal designs on it, and a bright-hilted sword. They wore red-embroidered hooded tunics.'

'I know them,' said Cú Chulainn. 'Those were Maine Athramail the Fatherlike and Maine Máithramail the Motherlike.'

'And this double wound,' said the doctor, 'was given to you by a father and son.'

'That's right,' said Cethern. 'Two great big men came at me with their eyes blazing. They wore helmets with gold horns. At their waists hung long swords, sheathed to their gold hilts in scabbards banded with gold fretwork.'

'I know them,' said Cú Chulainn. 'Those were Ailill and his son Maine Cotagaibi Uile, the Man of All Qualities.'

'What's the outlook for me, comrade Fíngin?' said Cethern.

'I won't lie to you,' said Fíngin. 'If I were you, I wouldn't be counting on my cows to calve. Had it been a case of only twos or threes, I might have been able to do something for you. As it is, you've taken a whole army of wounds, and your life is coming to an end, no matter what.'

Fíngin made to turn his chariot.

'Your sentence is the same as all the others,' said Cethern, and he dealt him such a blow with his fist that he sent him reeling across the shafts of the chariot and broke the chariot itself.

'That was a cruel kick to give an old man,' said Cú Chulainn (hence the name Uachtar Lúi, Kick Hill). 'You'd be better off battering your enemies, and not your doctors.'

On second thoughts the doctor gave Cethern a choice: either to treat his wounds for a year, after which he would live for whatever time would be left to him; or to treat him for three days and three nights so he would have enough strength to take on his enemies there and then. Cethern took the latter option.

The doctor instructed Cú Chulainn to get some bone-marrow for Cethern's cure. Cú Chulainn rustled up some cattle and made a mash of marrow out of their bones. Hence the name Smirromair, the Bath of Marrow, in Crích Rois.

Cethern slept day and night in the marrow, absorbing it. Then he said:

'My ribs are gone. Get me the ribs from the chariot-frame.'

'Consider it done,' said Cú Chulainn.

'If only I had my own weapons, what would I not do!' said Cethern. 'My deeds would be remembered for as many days as there are days to come.'

'What I see now looks very like what you are looking for,' said Cú Chulainn.

'What's that?' said Cethern.

'It looks like your wife Finn Bec is coming towards us in her chariot.'

No sooner said, than she appeared in front of them: Cethern's wife in a chariot chock-a-block with Cethern's weapons.

Cethern took his weapons, and then, with the ribs of the chariot strapped to his belly to support his body, Cethern went out to do battle with the enemy. Itholl, the doctor who'd been lying half-dead among the bodies of his fellow doctors, went ahead to warn the Connacht camp. Out of fear and trepidation they put Ailill's clothes and his crown on a pillar-stone to divert Cethern's rage when he arrived. Cethern went for the pillar-stone and drove his sword through it, and his fist after the sword. Hence the name Lia Toll, the Hole-Stone, in Crích Rois.

'A dirty trick!' said Cethern. 'I'll not rest till I see this crown on one of you!'

He fought them day and night until one of the Maine put on the crown and attacked him from his chariot. Cethern threw his shield at him: it cut him and his charioteer in halves, and ploughed through his horses into the ground. Then the army closed in on him. He killed all round him until he fell dead.

# XI
# SKIRMISHING

FINTAN, SON OF Niall Niamglonnach of the Dazzling Deeds, and the father of Cethern, came to avenge his son's death. He brought with him three fifties of battle-belted pikemen armed with double-headed pikes. Three times they engaged the enemy and they killed three times their own number, but in the end they were all killed. Afterwards, the lips and noses of their enemies were found protruding from the teeth of the corpses. Hence this battle is known as Fintan's Gnashing-Match.

Then Menn Mac Sálchada engaged Medb's forces with a band of thirty armed men. Twelve men of hers were killed by Menn and twelve of his were killed. Menn himself suffered deep wounds and was reddened with blood. And the men of Ireland said:

'Deep red is the shame of Menn Mac Sálchada – his followers slaughtered and destroyed, and he himself wounded and deep red with blood.'

Nevertheless they retreated from the camp before Menn, which is why he killed only twelve of them. He was told that they were not to blame for the deaths. They had gone nowhere near his home territory of the Boyne Waterways. And if he withdrew from their camp, there would be no shame on him, for it was understood that he would return with Conchobar when it came to the final battle, as predicted by the Irish druids. So Menn withdrew from the camp, and they withdrew a day's journey to the north.

Cú Chulainn sent his charioteer to Rochad Mac Faithemain of Ulster to ask him to come to his aid. As it happened, Medb's daughter Finnabair was in love with Rochad, who was the most handsome of the Ulster warriors. The charioteer went to Rochad and asked him, if he was over the Curse, to come and help Cú Chulainn. They planned to set a trap for the men of Ireland and kill them. Rochad came from the north with a hundred men and took up a position on a nearby height. The army saw him coming. Then Finnabair announced that Rochad was the man she had loved first, and loved above all others.

'Since you love him so much,' said Ailill and Medb, 'go and ask him for a truce until such times as he comes with Conchobar for the final battle. And spend the night with him.'

This was arranged, though Rochad was difficult to persuade. His tent was pitched beside Finnabair's, and he spent the night with her.

The Seven Munster Kings got to hear of this, and one of them said:

'The same girl was promised to me, on the guarantee of fifteen men, to get me to join this army.'

One by one the other six kings admitted that the same deal had been done with them. So they set off to vent their pique on Ailill's sons, who were guarding the rear of the army in the deep glen of Domain. Medb launched an attack on them, as did the three thousand Gailéoin, and Ailill, and Fergus. Seven hundred died in that mutual slaughter in the deep glen of Domain. When Finnabair heard that seven hundred men had died on her account, she dropped dead of shame. Hence the name Finnabair Sléibe, Finnabair of the Mountain.

Then Ilech went to take them on at Áth Feidli. He was the father of Connad Buide and the grandfather of Láegaire

Buadach. He was being looked after by his devoted grandson in Rath Impail when he announced that he'd take on the army and wreak his vengeance on them.

He set off in his decrepit chariot. It had neither rug nor cushion, and was hauled by two old sorrel hacks. He armed himself with his big rough shield of grey iron and his trusty blunt sword and his two rickety-headed rusty spears. And he loaded the chariot with clods and boulders and cobbles that he fired at anyone who came to stare at him and jeer him, stark naked as he was, with his long lad and his acorns dangling down through the floor of the chariot. And the army jeered him too when they saw him coming.

'If only,' they said, 'all the Ulstermen came to fight us like this.'

But Dóche Mac Mágach quelled their mockery. And in return Ilech told him that at the end of the day, when he had spent his strength fighting the army, Dóche could take his sword and cut off his head.

Then Ilech noticed the marrow-mash. He was told it had been made from Ulster cows' bones. So he made another marrow-mash beside it from Connachtmen's bones. At the end of the day Dóche cut off his head and brought it to his grandson Láegaire. He made peace with him, and Láegaire kept Ilech's sword.

Then the army advanced to Tailtiu. It was attacked by the charioteers of Ulster, three fifties of them. They killed three times their own number, and they themselves were killed. Roí Arad – Charioteers' Battlefield – is the name of the place where they died together on the Táin Bó Cúailnge.

One evening the army saw a great stone come flying towards them from the east and another just like it from the west. The two stones collided in mid-air and fell into the Irish camp. This performance went on until the same time the next day, with the army huddled together and holding their shields over

their heads to protect them against the missiles, till the whole
plain was littered with stones. Hence the name Mag Clochair,
Stony Plain.

It turned out that Cú Roí Mac Dáire was behind it: he
had come to help his people and was checked at Cotail by
Munremar Mac Gerrcin the Thick-necked, who had come to
Ard Róich from Emain Macha to help Cú Chulainn. Cú Roí
knew there was no one in the army who could withstand
Munremar. So between them Cú and Munremar carried on
this performance.

The army asked them to lay off. Munremar and Cú Roí
made peace. Cú Roí went home. Munremar went back to
Emain Macha, and did not return until the final battle.

While these events were taking place, Sualdam of Ráith Sualdaim in Muirthemne Plain heard how his son Cú Chulainn
had been under constant attack. And he said:

'Are the heavens rent? Does the sea leave its bed? Does the
earth open up? Or is this the cry of my son as he fights against
the odds?'

He went to his son. But the son was not pleased to see him.
True, he was badly wounded, but he knew his father would
not be strong enough to fight on anyone's account.

'Go to the men of Ulster,' said Cú Chulainn, 'and get them
to do battle with the army. If they do not, we will never be
avenged.'

Then his father saw that on Cú Chulainn's body there was
not so much as a spot that the tip of a rush couldn't cover
that wasn't pierced. Even the left hand, which was protected
by his shield, had fifty wounds in it. Sualdam went to Emain
Macha and cried out to the men of Ulster:

'Men murdered, women raped, cattle plundered!'

His first cry was from the side of the fort, his next from the
royal rampart, and his third from the Mound of Hostages
inside Emain itself.

No one answered, for among the Ulster people it was

not permissible to speak until Conchobar had spoken, and Conchobar would not speak until his druids had spoken. Then a druid said:

'Who rapes? Who plunders? Who murders?'.

'Ailill Mac Máta murders and rapes and plunders,' said Sualdam, 'aided and abetted by Fergus Mac Róich. Your people have been harassed as far as Dún Sobairche. Their cattle, their women and their herds have been carried off. Cú Chulainn has kept them out of Muirthemne and Crích Rois for the three months of winter. He's held together with bent hoops of wood, and dry wisps plug his wounds. Wounds that almost finished him off.'

'It would be appropriate,' said the druid, 'for a man who so provokes the king to die.'

'It would serve him right,' said Conchobar.

'And serve him right,' said the men of Ulster.

'What Sualdam says is true,' said Conchobar. 'Since the last Monday of summer to the first Monday of spring we've been raped and pillaged.'

Sualdam stormed out, dissatisfied with this response. He fell on to his shield and his head was cut off by the scalloped rim. His horse brought his head on the shield back to his house in Emain, and the head kept repeating the same warning.

'Truly, that is too powerful a cry,' said Conchobar, 'and I swear by the sea before them and the sky above them and the earth beneath them that I will restore every cow to its byre and every woman and child to their homes after victory in battle.'

Then Conchobar laid his hand on his son Finnchad Ferr Benn the Horned Man, so called because he wore silver horns. And he said:

'Arise, Finnchad! Go to Dedad in his inlet, to Leamain, to Fallach, to Illann Mac Fergusa, to Gabar, to Dorlunsa, to Imchlár, to Feidlimid Cilair Cétaig, to Fáeladán, to Rochaid Mac Faithemain at Rigdonn, to Lugaid, to Lugda, to Cathbath in his inlet, to the three Cairpres, to Aela, to Láeg at his

causeway, to Geimen in his valley, to Senoll Úathach at Diabul
Arda, to Cethern Mac Fintain at Carlag, to Torathor, to
Mulaig in his fortress, to the royal poet Aimirgin, to the
Úathadach Fodoblaid, to the Mórrigan at Dún Sobairche, to
Ieth, to Roth, to Fiachna at his mound, to Dam Dremed, to
Andiaraid, to Maine Mac Braitharge, to Dam Derg, to Mod,
to Maithes, to Irmaithes, to Corp Cliath, to Gabarleig in
Líne, to Eochaid Sainmech in Saimne, to Eochaid Lathach at
Latharna, to Uma Mac Remarbisi in Fedan, to Muinremur
Mac Gerrcind, to Senlobair at Canainn Gall, to Follomain,
to Lugaid rí Fer mBolc, to Laige Líne, to Búaidgalach, to
Ambúach, to Fergna, to Barrene, to Áine, to Errgi Echbél at
his hill, to Celtchar Mac Cuithechair in Lethglais, to Láegaire
Milbél at Breo Láegairi, to the three sons of Dromscalt Mac
Dregamm, to Drenda, to Drendas, to Cimb, to Cimling, to
Cimmene, to Fána Caba, to Fachtna Mac Senchath in his
rath, to Senchaid at Senchairthe, to Briccir, to Bricirne, to
Breic, to Buan, to Bairech, to Óengus Mac Leiti, to Fergus
Mac Leiti, to Óengus Fer mBolg, to Bruachur, to Alamiach
the warrior at Slánge, to the three sons of Fiachna in Cúailnge,
to Conall Cernach in Midlúachair, to Connad Mac Morna in
Callainn, to Cú Chulainn Mac Súaltaim in Muirthemne, to
Aimirgin at Eas Rúaid, to Lóeg, to Léiri, to Menn Mac Salch-
olca at Coirenna, to Cú Rí Mac Armargin in his rath, to
Óengus Fer Berm Umai, to Ogma Grianainech, to Brecc, to
Eo Mac Oircne, to Toillchenn, to Saithe, to Mogoll Echbél
in Magna, to Conla Sáeb, to Carba, to Láegaire Buadach in
Immail, to Alile Amargine in Tailtiu, to Furbaide Fer Benn,
to Seil, to Manes, to Cuscraid Menn Macha, to Fíngin at
Finngabra, to Cremath, to Blae Fichit, to Blae Brugaich, to
Fesair, to Eógan Mac Durthacht in Fernmag, to Ord, to
Seirid, to Serthe, to Oblán, to Cuilén, to Curether at Liana,
to Eithbenne, to Fernél, to Finnchath at Slíab Betha, to Talgo-
bain at Bernas, to Menn Mac Fer Calca, of Maig Dula, to
Íroll, to Bláirige at Tibraite Mac Ailchatha, to Ialla Ingraimme
of Mag Dobla, to Ros Mac Ailchatha, to Mane Mac Cruinn,

to Nindich Mac Cruinn, to Dipsemilid, to Mál Mac Roch-
raidi, to Muinne Mac Munremair, to Fiatach Fer nDoirre
Mac Dubthaig, to Muirne Menn.'

It was not difficult for Finnchad to deliver that summons,
for all the chieftains in Conchobar's province had been waiting for the word from Conchobar. From east and north and
west of Emain they came, and entered Emain to hear the news
that Conchobar had risen from his sick-bed. Then they struck
out southwards from Emain in search of the enemy. The first
stage of their march brought them to Iraird Cuillenn.

'Why are you waiting here?' said Conchobar.

'We're waiting for your sons,' said the Ulster army. 'They've
gone to Tara with three thousand men to contact Erc, the
Freckled Calf, son of Coirpre Nia Fer and Fedelm Noíchride.
We won't leave this spot until they return to join us.'

'Well, I'll not wait,' said Conchobar, 'for the men of Ireland
to find out that I've risen from my sick-bed, recovered from
the Curse.'

So Conchobar and Celtchar set off with three fifties of
chariots, and brought back eight score enemy heads from the
ford of Airthir Mide in East Meath. Hence its name now, Áth
Féne, Warrior Ford. These were the heads of men who had
been watching there for Conchobar's army. They also brought
back eight score women who had been held captive. When
Conchobar and Celtchar brought the heads to the camp
Celtchar said to Conchobar:

> ramparts awash     with blood     the king
> of slaughter     beyond compare     sundered
> body parts     the ground     surrendered
> to a hundred     streams     thirty four-horsed chariots
> steeds harnessed to     a hundred cruelties
> no want of leaders     two hundred druids
> a steadfast man     at Conchobar's back     prepare
> for battle     warriors     arise
> the battle     will erupt     at Gáirech and Ilgáirech

The same night Dubthach the Beetle of Ulster had a vision where he saw the army assembled at Gáirech and Ilgáirech. He spoke these words in his sleep:

> bewildering morning     bewildering times
> disordered armies     kings cast down
> necks broken     in the bloody sand
> three armies wiped out     by the Ulster army
> Conchobar at the heart     their women huddled
> herds driven     dawn after morning
> heroes cut down     hounds torn apart
> horses mangled     in the bloody mire
> as tribe     tramples tribe

This disturbed their sleep. The Nemain deranged the army. A hundred men fell dead. When everything was silent they heard Cormac Con Longes – or it might have been Ailill Mac Máta – chanting to the west of the camp:

> great the truce     the truce at Cuillenn
> great the plot     the plot at Delind
> great the cavalcade     the cavalcade at Assal
> great the torment     the torment at Tuath Bressi

# XII
# THE
# ULSTERMEN
# COME
# TOGETHER

WHILE THESE VISIONS were happening the men of Connacht, advised by Ailill and Medb and Fergus, decided to send scouts to see if the men of Ulster had reached the plain.

'Go, Mac Roth,' said Ailill, 'and find out if their men have arrived on the plain of Meath. As it is, I've taken all their goods and cattle. If they want a fight, they can have one. But if they haven't reached the plain, we'll be off.'

Mac Roth went out to scan the plain. He returned to Ailill and Medb and reported that when he first looked into the distance from Sliab Fúait he had seen all the beasts of the forest leaving their home and pouring out on to the plain.

'Then I took a second look,' said Mac Roth, 'and saw a thick mist filling the glens and valleys, so that the hills appeared like islands in a lake. I saw sparks of fire coming through the mist, sparks of every shade and colour in the world. Then there was a flash of lightning, and a great rumble of thunder, and a wind that nearly took the hair from my head and threw me on my back, though there's hardly a breeze today.'

'What is this, Fergus?' said Ailill. 'What can it mean?'

'I can tell you exactly what it means,' said Fergus. 'It's the men of Ulster, risen from their sick-beds. It was they who entered the forest. The vast number of their warriors and the violence of their passage shook the forest and caused the beasts of the forest to flee before them on to the plain. The thick mist that you saw was the breath of those powerful men filling the low ground so that the high ground appeared like islands in a lake. The lightning and the sparks of fire and the many colours that you saw, Mac Roth,' said Fergus, 'those were the eyes of the warriors flashing in their heads like sparks of fire. The thunder and the rumble and the clamour that you heard, that was the whirring of their swords and their ivory-hilted blades, their weapons rattling, chariots clattering, hoof-beats hammering, the shouts and roars and cries of chariot-fighters, warriors and soldiers, the ferocious rage and fury of heroes as they storm towards the battle. They're so fired up, they think they'll never get there.'

'We'll be waiting for them,' said Ailill. 'We have warriors to take them on.'

'You'll need them,' said Fergus, 'for no one – not in Ireland, nor the western world from Greece and Scythia westwards to the Orkney Islands and the Pillars of Hercules, as far as Breogan's Tower and the Isles of Gades – can withstand the men of Ulster in their battle-fury.'

Mac Roth set off again to gauge the advance of the Ulstermen and went as far as their camp at Slane in Meath. He reported back to Ailill and Medb and Fergus, giving them a detailed account of what he had seen.

'A great company came to the hill at Slane in Meath,' said Mac Roth, 'proud and powerful and battle-hungry. I'd put their numbers at about three thousand. Without further ado they stripped down and dug a mound of sods as a throne for their leader. He was a most impressive, regal figure as he led that company, slim, tall and handsome, with finely cut blond hair falling down in waves and curls between his shoulder-blades. He wore a pleated shirt of royal purple and a red-embroidered white hooded tunic. A dazzling brooch of red gold was pinned to the breast of his mantle. His grey eyes had a calm gaze. His face was ruddy-cheeked, with a broad brow and a fine jaw. He had a forked beard of golden curls. Slung across his shoulders was a sword with a gold pommel and a bright shield inlaid with animal designs. He held a slender-shafted spear with a blued steel head. His retinue was the finest of any prince on earth, a fearsome and formidable body of men, magnificently equipped, whose bearing spoke of triumph, rage, implacable resolve and dignity.

'Another company came up,' said Mac Roth, 'almost as impressive as the first in terms of numbers, bearing, dress and fierce resolve. A handsome young hero led that company. He wore a bordered knee-length tunic and a green cloak fastened at the shoulder with a gold brooch. He had a head of curly yellow hair. An ivory-hilted sword hung at his left side, and he carried a deadly scallop-edged shield. In his hand was a spear like a palace torch-standard, with three silver rings around it that ran freely up and down the shaft from grip to tip and back again. The company took up a position to the left of the first company, with knee to ground and shield-rim held to chin. I detected a stammer in the speech of the great stern warrior who led that company.

'Another company came up,' said Mac Roth. 'I'd put their numbers at above three thousand. A brave, handsome, broad-faced man was at their head. He had wavy brown hair and a long, forked, wispy beard. He wore a white knee-length hooded tunic and dark-grey fringed cloak pinned at the breast with a leaf-shaped brooch of white bronze. He carried a shield inlaid with animal designs in many colours. At his waist hung a sword with a domed silver pommel, and he held a five-pronged spear in his hand. He sat down facing the leader of the first company.'

'Who were they, Fergus?' said Ailill.

'I know them well,' said Fergus. 'Conchobar, king of a province of Ireland, is the one who was seated on the mound of sods. Seancha Mac Ailill, the most eloquent man in Ulster, is the one who sat facing him. And Cúscraid Menn Macha the Stammerer, Conchobar's son, is the one who sat by his father's side. As for those three rings around his spear, they only run up and down like that before a victory. And as for

the companies assembled there, these are men you can count
on to do great damage in any battle,' said Fergus.

'They'll find men to answer them here,' said Medb.

'I swear by the gods my people swear by,' said Fergus, 'that
the army has not been raised in Ireland that could withstand
the men of Ulster.'

'Another company came up,' said Mac Roth, 'more than
three thousand of them, led by a big strong warrior, swarthy,
fiery-faced and fearsome, with a glib of brown hair plastered
to his forehead. He carried a curved scallop-edged shield. He
held a five-pronged spear and a forked javelin besides. A
bloodstained sword was slung on his back. He wore a white
knee-length tunic, and a purple cloak pinned at the shoulder
with a gold brooch.'

'Who was that, Fergus?' said Ailill.

'A man built for battle,' said Fergus, 'first to the fray, the
doom of enemies: Eoghan Mac Durthacht, King of Fernmag.'

'Another powerful and imperious company came to the hill
at Slane in Meath,' said Mac Roth, 'harbingers of dread and
terror, their cloaks thrown back behind them, marching res-
olutely towards the hill with a fearsome clattering of arms.
Their leader was a grim-looking fellow with a thick-set,
grizzled head and big yellow eyes. He was wrapped in a yellow
cloak with a white border. A deadly scalloped-edged shield
hung by his side. In one hand he held a long, broad-bladed
spear; in the other he held its match, the blade stained with
the blood of his enemies. A long, lethal sword was slung
across his shoulders.'

'Who was that, Fergus?' said Ailill.

'A warrior who never turns his back on battle: Láegaire
Buadach the Victorious, son of Connad son of Ilech from
Impail in the north,' said Fergus.

'Another great company came to the hill at Slane in Meath,'
said Mac Roth, 'headed by a fine-looking, barrel-chested,
thick-necked warrior. He had ruddy cheeks, a shock of black
curls and flashing grey eyes. He wore a cloak of brown shaggy

wool pinned with a bright silver brooch. He carried a black shield with a bronze boss. A spear with a needle's-eye head glittered in his hand. The ivory pommel of his sword sat proud against his red-embroidered braided tunic.'

'Who was that, Fergus?' said Ailill.

'The instigator of many battles. A tidal wave that overwhelms little streams. A man of three cries. The vicious doom of enemies,' said Fergus. 'Munremar Mac Gerrcinn the Thick-Necked, from Moduirn in the north.'

'Another great company came to the hill at Slane in Meath,' said Mac Roth, 'a most impressive company, their cohorts well drilled and splendidly kitted out. They marched imperiously up to the hill. The clatter of their arms as they advanced shook everyone. They were led by a majestic warrior, superlative among men for his hair and eyes and grim demeanour, for dress and build and clarity of voice, for dignity and grandeur and gracefulness, for range and style of fighting skills, for equipment, application and discernment, for honour and nobility of lineage.'

'You have him in a nutshell,' said Fergus. 'That brilliant figure is Feidlimid the Handsome, the raging warrior, the overwhelming wave, the irresistible force, who comes home in triumph after slaughtering his enemies abroad: Feidlimid Cilair Cétaig.'

'Another company came to the hill at Slane in Meath,' said Mac Roth, 'at least three thousand strong, led by a big, stalwart warrior, sallow-complexioned, with a head of black curls and a haughty stare in his grey eyes. A great, rugged bull of a man. He wore a white hooded tunic and a grey cloak with a silver pin at the shoulder. A sword hung at his hip, and he carried a red shield with a hammered silver boss. The spear in his hand had a broad blade and triple rivets.'

'Who was that, Fergus?' said Ailill.

'A furious flame, bold in battle, a man who wins wars: Connad Mac Morna from Callann,' said Fergus.

'Another company came to the hill at Slane in Meath,' said

Mac Roth, 'a veritable army of them. As for the leader of that vast force, seldom will you find a warrior so poised and stylishly equipped. His auburn hair was neatly trimmed, his handsome, well-proportioned face aglow. Finely shaped red lips, pearl-white teeth, a firm, clear voice: every aspect of him was superlative. Draped over his red-embroidered hooded tunic was a purple cloak with an inlaid gold brooch. At his left side hung a silver-bossed shield inlaid with animal designs in many colours. In one hand he held a spear with a head of blued steel; in the other hand he held a deadly sharp dagger. A gold-hilted golden sword was slung on his back.'

'Who was that, Fergus?' said Ailill.

'Someone well known to us,' said Fergus. 'A man equal to an army, tenacious as a bloodhound, a deciding factor in any combat: Rochad Mac Faithemain from Brig Dumae, your son-in-law, who took your daughter Finnabair.'

'Another company came to the hill at Slane in Meath,' said Mac Roth, 'led by a feisty-looking, dark-haired warrior with brawny legs and bulging thighs. Each of his four limbs was as thick as a man. He was every inch a man, and more,' said Mac Roth. 'He had a scarred, purple face and haughty, blood-shot eyes: a formidable, bustling man, alert and dangerous, his entourage equipped and kitted out in admirable fashion; a proud, aggressive man, whose scorn and anger drives him into battle against overwhelming odds to beat his enemies, who ventures unprotected into hostile territory – no wonder his company marched so boldly to the hill at Slane in Meath.'

'A brave warlike man indeed,' said Fergus, 'hot-blooded, tough, vehement and dignified, a force to be reckoned with in any army: my own foster-brother, Fergus Mac Leiti, King of Líne, battle-spearhead of the north of Ireland.'

'Another great imposing company came to the hill at Slane in Meath,' said Mac Roth. 'They were wonderfully equipped. At their head was a fine, tall figure of a man with brilliant hair and eyes and skin, magnificently proportioned. He held himself with immense aplomb. He wore five gold chains, a green cloak pinned at the shoulder with a gold brooch, and a white hooded tunic. In his hand was a spear like the turret of a palace. A gold-hilted sword was slung on his back.'

'Fearsome and formidable indeed the same conquering hero,' said Fergus. 'That was Amargin son of Eiccet Salach the smith, from Buais in the north.'

'Another company came to the hill at Slane in Meath,' said Mac Roth, 'a veritable torrent of them, a raging fire, a pride of lions, their number legion, marching in a huge, cliff-like, rock-steady, doom-laden, brutal, thunderous wave. At their head was a grim, coarse-faced warrior, big-bellied, thick-lipped, with a shock of grizzled hair, and a great big nose, and red arms and legs. He wore a rough woolly tunic and a stripy cloak pinned with an iron spike. He carried a curved scallop-edged shield and a big spear with a head of blued steel and thirty rivets in it. A sword tempered seven times by fire hung from his shoulders. The whole army rose up to greet him in a ripple of disarray as he approached the hill.'

'A supreme champion in battle,' said Fergus. 'A man equal to an army. A furious force, a stormy wave that pours over its boundaries: Celtchar Mac Uthidir from Dún Lethglaise in the north.'

'Another company came to the hill at Slane in Meath,' said Mac Roth. 'They were led by a dazzling warrior in a white outfit that matched his albino hair and eyelashes and beard. He carried a shield with a golden boss, an ivory-hilted sword, and a spear with a broad needle's-eye head. Bravely indeed did that warrior advance.'

'That was our own, dear, splendid bear, whose blows are irresistible,' said Fergus, 'a magnificent crusher of his enemies: Feredach Finn Fechtnach, from the grove at Sliab Fúait in the north.'

'Another company came to the hill at Slane in Meath,' said Mac Roth, 'led by an ugly, big-bellied warrior with huge lips – they were as big as a horse's lips. He had dark curly hair, a broad, mottled face and long arms. He wore a loose black cloak pinned with a bronze annular brooch. He held a dark blue shield at his left side. In his right hand was a massive banded spear. A long sword was slung on his back.'

'A ferocious lion, red in claw,' said Fergus, 'all-powerful and unstoppable as he scorches the earth: Eirrge Echbél the horse-lipped, from Brí Eirrge in the north.'

'Another company came to the hill at Slane in Meath,' said Mac Roth, 'led by two handsome young heroes, yellow-haired, alike in looks and age. They carried bright shields with animal designs on them. Together they lifted their feet and together they set them down, each in perfect step with the other.'

'Who are they, Fergus?' said Ailill.

'Two warriors, two bright flames, two spearheads,' said Fergus, 'two champions and pillars of the fray, two dragons, two fires, two fighters, two bold battle-shafts, the two pets of Ulster and its king: Fiachna and Fiacha, the two dear sons of Conchobar Mac Nessa, and the two darlings of the north of Ireland.'

'Another company came to the hill at Slane in Meath,' said Mac Roth, 'led by three forceful, fiery, purple-faced warriors, each with a poll of yellow hair. All three wore red-embroidered sleeved tunics and uniform cloaks pinned at the shoulder with a gold brooch. They carried uniform shields. Each had a gold-hilted sword on his back and a broad bright spear in his hand. All three looked equally experienced.'

'Those are the three conquerors from Cuib, the three mighty men of Mídluachair, the three princes of Roth, the three veterans from the East End of Sliab Fúait,' said Fergus, 'the three sons of Fiachna: Rus, Dáire and Imchad, who have come to take back the Bull.'

'Another company came to the hill at Slane in Meath,' said Mac Roth, 'led by a quick, passionate man with fierce, glowing eyes. He wore a white, knee-length, hooded tunic and a tabby cloak with an annular brooch. He had a grey shield on his left arm, and at his hip hung a sword with a silver pommel.

In his vengeful right hand was a death-dealing spear. His men were bloodstained and wounded, and he himself was scarred and bleeding.'

'That,' said Fergus, 'is one ruthless warrior. He tears into battle like a wild boar or a goaded bull. He is the conqueror from Baile, the man in the gap, the all-consuming blaze from Colptha, stern guardian of the portal to the north of Ireland: Menn Mac Salchada from Corann. He has come here to avenge his wounds,' said Fergus.

'Another company came to the hill at Slane in Meath,' said Mac Roth, 'a spirited and battle-hungry force. Their leader was a sallow, long-cheeked warrior with a head of bushy brown hair. He wore a handsome tunic and a fine red woollen cloak held at the shoulder by a gold pin. At his left hung a splendid sword with a gleaming silver pommel. He carried a red shield and a fine ash-handled spear with a broad head of blued steel.'

'That was a man of three death-dealing strokes,' said Fergus, 'a man of three roads and three highways and three byways, a man of three accomplishments and three cries, who breaks his enemies in battle beyond the borders: Fergna Mac Finnchoíme, from Corann.'

'Another company came to the hill at Slane in Meath,' said Mac Roth, 'upwards of three thousand of them, led by a handsome, broad-chested warrior, very like Ailill yonder in looks and build and gear. He had a gold helmet on his head. He wore a red-embroidered tunic and a beautiful cloak pinned at the breast with a gold brooch. He carried a gold-rimmed, double-dealing shield and a spear like a palace turret. A gold-hilted sword was slung on his back.'

'He is the sea against a stream,' said Fergus. 'He is an all-consuming blaze. His rage against his enemies is irresistible: Ferbaide Fer Benn, the Horned Man.'

'Another company came to the hill at Slane in Meath,' said Mac Roth, 'countless numbers of heroes wearing strange outfits, very different to the other companies. With all their

gear and weapons and equipment they made a marvellous
spectacle as they advanced. They were an army in themselves.
At their head was a bright-faced, freckled, perfectly formed
little boy. He held a gold-studded, gold-rimmed shield with a
white boss and a shimmering, keen-bladed light javelin. He
wore a red-embroidered white hooded tunic and a purple
fringed cloak held at the breast with a silver pin. A gold-hilted
sword sat proud against his garments.'

Fergus paused before he spoke.

'I don't know,' said Fergus, 'of any boy among the Ulster
people who would fit that description. These must be the men
of Tara, and this must be the fine and noble Erc, son of
Coirpre Niad Fer and Conchobar's daughter. There's no love
lost between Coirpre and Conchobar, and the boy must have
come to his grandfather's aid without the permission of his
father. Because of that young lad,' said Fergus, 'you will lose
the battle. He will plunge fearlessly into the heart of the fray,
and the warriors of Ulster will raise a great shout as they rush
forward, cutting down your army before them to rescue their
beloved little calf. They will all feel the ties that bind them
when they see the boy under attack. Then will be heard the
whirr of Conchobar's sword, like the growl of a bloodhound,
as he comes to save the boy. Conchobar will cast up three
ramparts of dead men around the battlefield in the search for
his grandson. And, moved by the ties that bind them, the
warriors of Ulster will descend on your vast army.'

'I have been overlong,' said Mac Roth, 'in describing everything I saw. But I thought I should let you know what was
going on.'

'You have certainly done that,' said Fergus.

'However,' said Mac Roth, 'Conall Cernach did not come
with his great company. Nor did Conchobar's three sons,
with their three divisions. Nor did Cú Chulainn come, for he
was wounded fighting against the odds. But many hundreds
and thousands converged on the Ulster camp. Many heroes,
champions and warriors came racing on their horses to that

great meeting. And many more companies were still arriving as I left. Wherever I cast my eye,' said Mac Roth, 'on any hill or height from Fer Diad's Ford to Slane in Meath, all I could see was men and horses.'

'What you saw was a people coming together,' said Fergus.

# XIII
# THE
# FINAL
# BATTLE

CONCHOBAR CAME WITH his forces and camped beside the others. He asked Ailill for a truce until sunrise. Ailill consented on behalf of the men of Ireland and the Ulster exiles, and Conchobar consented on behalf of the men of Ulster. The men of Ireland pitched their tents, and before the sun had set there was hardly a bare piece of ground between them and the Ulstermen. In the twilight between the two camps the Morrígan spoke:

> ravens gnaw    men's necks    blood gushes
> fierce fray    hacked flesh    battle-drunk
> men's sides    blade-struck    war-torn
> raking fingers    battle-brave    men of Crúachan
> ruination    bodies crushed    underfoot
> long live Ulster    woe to Ireland
> woe to Ulster    long live Ireland

These last words – 'woe to Ulster' – she conveyed to the ears of the men of Ireland, to make them think the war was as good as won. That night Nét's consorts, Nemain and the Badb, began howling at the men of Ireland, and a hundred warriors dropped dead of fright. It was not the most peaceful of nights for them.

On the eve of the battle Ailill Mac Mata chanted:

'Rise up, Traighthrén, powerful of foot. Summon for me the three Conaires from Sliab Mis, the three Lussens from

Lúachair, the three Niad Chorb from Tilach Loiscthe, the three Dóelfers from Dell, the three Dámaltachs from Dergderc, the three Bodars from the Buas, the three Baeths from the river Buaidnech, the three Búageltachs from Mag mBreg, the three Suibnes from the river Suir, the three Eochaids from Ane, the three Malleths from Loch Erne, the three Abatruads from Loch Ríb, the three Mac Amras from Ess Rúaid, the three Fiachas from Fid Nemain, the three Maines from Mureisc, the three Muredachs from Mairg, the three Loegaires from Lecc Derg, the three Brodonns from the river Barrow, the three Brúchnechs from Cenn Abrat, the three Descertachs from Druim Fornacht, the three Finns from Finnabair, the three Conalls from Collamair, the three Carbres from Cliu, the three Maines from Mossa, the three Scáthglans from Scaire, the three Echtaths from Erce, the three Trénfers from Taite, the three Fintans from Femen, the three Rótanachs from Raigne, the three Sárchorachs from Suide Lagen, the three Etarscéls from Étarbán, the three Aeds from Aidne, the three Guaires from Gabal.'

These Triads, as they were known, had survived Cú Chulainn's attacks on the Irish army.

Meanwhile Cú Chulainn was close by at Fedain Collna. His supporters would bring him food by night, and talk things over with him by day. He killed no one north of Fer Diad's Ford.

'Some cattle have strayed from the western camp to the eastern camp,' his charioteer said to Cú Chulainn, 'and look, a party of young fellows have gone out to round them up. What's more, a party of our own young fellows have gone after the cattle too.'

'The two lots of young fellows will clash,' said Cú Chulainn, 'and they'll be joined by others who will give no quarter. The cattle will stray all the more.'

It happened as Cú Chulainn said it would.

'How are the Ulster boys fighting?' said Cú Chulainn.

'Like men,' said the charioteer.

'The same boys would be proud to die for their herd,' said Cú Chulainn. 'And now?'

'The beardless youngsters have joined them now,' said the charioteer.

'Is there any ray of sunlight yet?' said Cú Chulainn.

'Not a glimmer,' said the charioteer.

'If only I was fit to go and help them,' said Cú Chulainn.

'Now the real fighting begins,' said the charioteer as the sun came up. 'The higher echelons are going into battle, except the kings, for they are asleep.'

As the sun came up, Fachtna spoke (or maybe it was Conchobar, chanting in his sleep):

> Arise     brave kings of Macha     generous people
> sharpen swords     wage war     dig in
> strike shields     arms weary     bellowing herds
> of men     in rightful strife     battle ranks
> their reign     brought down     by fighting men
> as enemies     ambush     killing all day
> imbibing     deep draughts     of blood
> the hearts     of queens     swelling
> with grief     and blood     soaks
> the trampled grass     whereon     they stand
> and fall     arise     kings of Macha

'Who chanted that?' said they all.

'Conchobar Mac Nessa,' said some.

'Fachtna,' said others.

'Sleep on, sleep on, but still keep watch!'

And Láegaire Buadach the Victorious said:

> Beware     kings of Macha
> ready swords     to guard     what cattle

> you have plundered    drive    the Connachtmen
> from Uisnech Hill    body    torque-twisted
> sinews blazing    he will strike    the world
> on the plain of Gáirech

'Who chanted that?' said they all.
'Láegaire Buadach, son of Connad Buide son of Iliach. Sleep on, sleep on, but still keep watch!'
'Wait a little longer,' said Conchobar, 'till the sun has risen well above the hills and glens of Ireland.'
When Cú Chulainn saw the western kings putting on their crowns and rallying their troops, he told his charioteer to rouse up the men of Ulster.
The charioteer spoke – or maybe it was the poet Amargin Mac Eicit:

> Arise    brave kings of Macha
> generous people    the Badb    lusts after
> Impail cattle    heart's blood    pouring forth
> as men pour in    to battle    brave deeds
> heads skewed    in flight    bogged down
> in blood    and battle-weariness    for there is
> no one    like Cú Chulainn    to enforce
> the will of Macha    all for    Cúailnge cattle
> arise    kings of Macha

'I've roused them up,' said the charioteer. 'They've charged into battle stark naked,[1] wearing nothing but their weapons. Any man whose tent door was facing east, he's gone westward through his tent for a shortcut.'
'Speedy help in time of need,' said Cú Chulainn.
After a while, he said:
'Take a look for us, comrade Láeg, and tell us how the men of Ulster are fighting.'
'Bravely,' said the charioteer. 'If Conall Cernach's charioteer Én[2] and myself were to drive from one wing of the battle

to the other, not a wheel nor a hoof would touch ground, so closely do they fight.'

'This has the makings of a great encounter,' said Cú Chulainn. 'Whatever happens in the battle, be sure to let me know about it.'

'I'll do my level best,' said the charioteer.

'Right now the western warriors have broken through the eastern battle-line,' he said.

'And now the eastern warriors have broken through the western battle-line.'

'If only I were fit,' said Cú Chulainn, 'you'd see me breaking through along with the rest.'

The Irish Triads began to advance towards the battle at Gáirech and Ilgáirech. Accompanying them were the nine chariot-fighters from Iruath, each preceded by three foot-soldiers keeping pace with the chariots. Medb was keeping them in reserve to take Ailill out of harm's way if they were beaten, or to kill Conchobar if they won.

Then the charioteer told Cú Chulainn that Ailill and Medb were pressurizing Fergus to go into battle, saying that it was only right that he should do so, after all that they had done for him during his exile.

'If only I had my own sword,' said Fergus, 'the soldiers' heads I'd cut off would bounce off their shields like hailstones into the mud churned up by the king's horses as they plough through the battlefield.'

And he swore this oath:

'I swear by the god my people swear by, that I'd strike jaws from necks, necks from shoulders, shoulders from elbows, elbows from forearms, forearms from fists, fists from fingers, fingers from nails; crowns from skulls, skulls from trunks, trunks from thighs, thighs from calves, calves from feet, feet from toes, and toes from nails. Heads would fly from necks like bees buzzing to and fro on a fine day.'

Then Ailill said to his charioteer:

'Bring me the sword that violates flesh. I swear the oath of

my people that if it has lost any of its bloom since the day I
gave it to you on that wet hill-slope in Ulster, all of Ireland
will not save you from me.'

The sword was brought to Fergus and Ailill said:

> take your sword    though once    you struck out
> at Ireland    one of her sons    a mighty hero
> will fight at Gáirech    if this be    the truth
> for the sake of    your honour    wreak not
> your wrath    on us but on    Ulster's chariot-warriors
> at dawn    at Gáirech    the field sodden
> with the deep    red morning

Fergus said:

> well met    Harshblade    Léte's³ sword
> the Badb's swift messenger    of doom
> and horror    no longer concealed    come
> avenge    and sever    sinews
> topple heads    this sword    no longer
> in a king's keeping    the story    to be told
> again    I take    my kingly stance
> before the men    of Ireland

'A pity indeed, were you to fall in the thick of battle,' said
Fergus to Ailill.

Fergus seized his weapons and went towards the fighting.
Wielding his sword in both hands, he took out a hundred
men. Medb also seized her weapons and plunged into the
fray. Three times she cleared all before her until she was
repelled by a thicket of spears.

'I'd like to know,' said Conchobar to his companions, 'who
it is that's taking the battle to us in the north. Hold the line
here and I'll go and seek him out.'

'We'll stick to this spot,' said the warriors, 'and unless the ground opens up under us, or the heavens fall on us, we'll not give an inch.'

Then Conchobar went to meet Fergus. He raised his shield against him – the shield Óchaín, the Dazzling Ear, with its four gold spikes and four gold plates. Fergus dealt it three blows, but the rim of the shield did not even touch Conchobar's head.

'Who is the Ulsterman that holds this shield?' said Fergus.

'A better man than you,' said Conchobar. 'One who drove you into exile to dwell among the wolves and foxes; one who by dint of his deeds will repel you before all the men of Ireland.'

With that, Fergus raised his sword in a two-handed grip, intending to deal Conchobar a vengeful blow. As the point of his sword touched the ground on the backswing, Cormac Mac Loinges gripped his arm with his two hands and said:

> reckless     careful
> comrade Fergus     too considered
> ill considered     comrade Fergus
> friend     becoming foe
> behold     your enemies
> the friends     you forsook
> as you prepare     to strike
> these wicked blows     comrade Fergus

'What then should I do?' said Fergus.

'Strike out at those three hills yonder. Turn your hand. Strike anywhere. Be as reckless as you like. But remember that the honour of Ulster has never been compromised, and never will be, unless by you today.'

'Come away from here, Conchobar,' said Cormac to his father. 'This man will no longer vent his rage on Ulstermen.'

Fergus turned round and in a single onslaught cut down a hundred Ulstermen with his sword. He came up against Conall Cernach.

'You're very fierce,' said Conall, 'against your own kith and kin, and all for the sake of a whore's backside.'

'What then should I do?' said Fergus.

'Strike out at those hills yonder, and anything on top of them,' said Conall.

Fergus struck the hills and with three blows sheared off the tops of the Máela Midi, the Flat-topped Hills of Meath.

Cú Chulainn heard the blows which Fergus dealt the hills, just as he heard those struck on Conchobar's shield.

'Who strikes those tremendous blows in the distance?' said Cú Chulainn,

> the heart swells with blood
> rage sunders the world
> quick, undo the hoops

Láeg answered:

'Those blows were struck by the bold and dauntless Fergus Mac Róich. A man who is a byword for much blood and slaughter. His sword was hidden in the chariot-shaft in the event of Conchobar's horse-soldiers joining the war.'

And Cú Chulainn said:

> quick, undo the hoops
> men covered in blood
> swords to be wielded
> lives to be cut short

Then the dry wisps which had plugged his wounds soared up into the air like skylarks and the hoops around him sprang asunder and bits of them landed as far away as Mag Tuag – the Plain of the Hoops – in Connacht. They flew away from him in all directions. The blood in his wounds began to boil. He knocked together the heads of the two women who had been watching over him so that each was spattered with grey from the other's brains. These were two handmaidens sent by

Medb to make a show of sorrow over him, so that his wounds would open afresh, and to tell him that Ulster had been beaten and Fergus killed in battle because Cú Chulainn was not fit to join the fight. Then the Torque seized him. The twenty-seven leather corsets he would wear going into battle, lashed to his body with ropes and thongs, were now brought to him. He took up his chariot on his back – frame, wheels and all – and walked the battle-field in search of Fergus.

'Over here, comrade Fergus,' said Cú Chulainn.

Three times he called him. Three times there was no answer.

'I swear by the god of the Ulstermen,' said Cú Chulainn, 'that I'll thrash you like flax in a pond! I'll rear up on you like a tail over a cat! I'll spank you the way a fond mother spanks her wee boy!'

'Who's the Irishman who speaks to me like that?' said Fergus.

'Cú Chulainn, son of Sualdam and Conchobar's sister,' said Cú Chulainn. 'Now yield to me.'

'I did promise that once,' said Fergus.

'Then give what's due,' said Cú Chulainn.

'All right, so,' said Fergus. 'You yielded to me once, and now look at you, all full of holes.'

So Fergus left the field and took his three thousand men with him. The Gailéoin and the men of Munster left too. Nine divisions of three thousand – those of Medb and Ailill and their seven sons – were left in the battle. It was noon when Cú Chulainn joined the fray. By the time the sun had brushed the tops of the trees, he had scattered the last of their companies, and all that remained of his chariot was a handful of ribs from the frame and a handful of spokes from the wheels.

Medb covered the retreat of the men of Ireland. She sent the Donn Cúailnge on to Crúachan along with fifty of his heifers and eight of her messengers, so that the Bull would arrive there, as she had sworn.

Then Medb got her gush of blood.

'Fergus,' she said, 'cover the retreat of the men of Ireland, for I must relieve myself.'

'By god,' said Fergus, 'you picked a bad time to go.'

'I can't help it,' said Medb. 'I'll die if I don't go.'

So Fergus covered the retreat. Medb relieved herself, and it made three great trenches, each big enough for a cavalcade. Hence the place is known as Fúal Medba, Medb's Piss-pot.

Cú Chulainn came upon Medb as she was doing what she had to.

'I'm at your mercy,' said Medb.

'If I were to strike, and kill you,' said Cú Chulainn, 'I'd be within my rights.'

But he spared her, because usually he did not kill women. He escorted them west until they crossed the ford of Áth Luain. He struck three blows with his sword at the nearby hills, which are now known as Máelana Átha Luain, the Flat-topped Hills of Athlone: this was his response to the Flat-topped Hills of Meath.

Now that they had lost the battle, Medb said to Fergus:

'The pot was stirred, Fergus, and today a mess was made.'[4]

'That's usually what happens,' said Fergus, 'when a mare leads a herd of horses – all their energy gets pissed away, following the rump of a skittish female.'

The Donn Cúailnge was brought to Connacht. When he saw this strange and beautiful new land he let three great bellows out of him. Finnbennach, the White-horned Bull, heard him. On account of Finnbennach no male beast on the Plain of Aí dared raise a sound louder than a moo. He threw up his head and proceeded to Crúachan to seek out the Brown Bull. Everyone who had escaped the battle now had nothing better to do than to watch the two bulls fighting.

The men of Ireland debated as to who should referee the contest of the two bulls. They agreed it should be Bricriu Mac Carbada the Venom-tongued. A year before the events narrated in the Táin, Bricriu had gone from one province to the other to negotiate some deal or other with Fergus. Fergus took him into his employ until such times as his possessions would arrive. They were playing chess when they had a difference of opinion, and Bricriu insulted Fergus rather badly. Fergus struck him on the head with the chessman he had been holding and broke a bone in his skull. So Bricriu had lain recuperating while the men of Ireland went forth on the Táin. The day they returned, he got up from his sick-bed. They chose Bricriu because he did not discriminate between friend and foe. They brought him to the gap between the bulls to referee the contest.

When the two bulls saw each other they pawed the ground and hurled the earth over their shoulders. Their eyes blazed in their heads like great fiery orbs and their cheeks and their nostrils swelled like forge bellows. They charged towards each other and Bricriu got caught in between. He was flattened, trampled and killed. Such was the death of Bricriu.

The Brown Bull got his hoof stuck on his opponent's horn. For a day and a night he made no attempt to withdraw the hoof, until Fergus gave off to him and took a stick to his hide.

'It would be a poor show,' said Fergus, 'for this feisty old calf to be brought all this way only to disgrace his fine breeding. Especially since so many died on his account.'

When the Brown Bull heard this he pulled away his hoof and broke his leg. The other bull's horn flew off and stuck in the side of a nearby mountain. Hence the name Sliab nAdarca, Horn Mountain.

The bulls fought for a long time. Night fell upon the men of Ireland and they could do nothing but listen to the bulls roaring and bellowing in the darkness. All next day the Donn Cúailnge drove Finnbennach before him and at nightfall they plunged into the lake at Crúachan. He emerged with Finnbennach's loins and shoulderblade and liver on his horns. The army went to kill him but Fergus stopped them, saying he should be let roam. So the Bull headed for his homeland. He stopped on the way to drink at Finnleithe, where he left Finnbennach's shoulderblade. Hence the name Finnleithe,

White Shoulder. He drank again at Áth Luain, and left Finnbennach's loins there. Hence the name Áth Luain, the Ford of the Loins. At Iraird Cuillenn he let a great bellow out of him that was heard all over the province. He drank again at Tromma, where Finnbennach's liver fell from his horns. Hence the name Tromma, Liver. He went then to Éten Tairb, where he rested his brow against the hill. Hence the name Éten Tairb, the Bull's Brow, in Muirthemne Plain. Then he went by the Midluachair Road to Cuib, where he used to dwell with the dry cows of Dáire, and he tore up the ground there. Hence the name Gort mBúraig, Trench Field. Then he went on and fell dead at the ridge between Ulster and Uí Echach. That place is now called Druim Tairb, Bull Ridge.

Ailill and Medb made a peace with the Ulstermen and Cú Chulainn. For seven years after that no one was killed in battle between them. The men of Connacht went back to their own country, and the men of Ulster returned in triumph to Emain Macha.

# FINIT
# AMEN

# NOTES

DIL = *Dictionary of the Irish Language,* Royal Irish Academy, Dublin 1998

## I THE PILLOW TALK AND ITS OUTCOME

1.  *Ailill:* A name with an original meaning of 'brilliant one' or 'phantom', a designation of an ancestor-deity in some contexts.
2.  *Medb:* The name means 'intoxicator', cognate with English 'mead'. She is seen by some commentators as an echo of an ancient sovereignty goddess.
3.  *Crúachan:* 'Place of mounds'. Identified today as a site near Rathcroghan in County Roscommon, covering 518 hectares and containing some seventy archaeological features, including twenty ring-forts, burial mounds and megalithic tombs. There is an interpretative centre in the nearby village of Tulsk.
4.  *for every soldier of them I had ten, and for every ten I had nine more . . . and one:* The computation is rhetorical. According to R. A. S. Macalister (*Ancient Ireland*, London: 1935), 'If Queen Medb really said this, I am afraid we must accuse her majesty of overstatement; for the retinue specified amounts to 40,478,703,000 persons.'
5.  *Conchobar:* The name, literally, means 'hound-lover'. In the *Táin* and other stories Conchobar is usually presented as an attractive figure. However, he is the villain of the piece in 'The Exile of the Sons of Uisliu' (see p. 210, note 1 to Cormac Conn Longas). In *Compert Conchoboir* ('The Begetting of Conchobar') we are told that one day Nes the daughter of Eochaid

Sálbuide is encountered by the druid Cathbad. She asks him what that hour might be favourable for. 'For begetting a king on a queen,' he replies. 'Really?' says Nes. Cathbad swears that it is true, and since no other man is about she takes Cathbad. A boy, Conchobar, is born of their union. At this time the king of Ulster is Fergus Mac Róich. When Conchobar reaches the age of seven Fergus takes a fancy to Nes. She agrees to sleep with him if she gets something in return, namely, to give her son the kingship of Ulster for a year. The bargain is struck. While her son is king in name, she gets her household to steal everything from one half of her people and give it to the other half, and she gives all her gold and silver to the Ulster warriors. When the year is up the Ulstermen debate what to do. They feel insulted that Fergus has given them over like a dowry, while they are grateful to Conchobar for all they received from him. So Fergus is deposed, Cathbad's son Conchobar takes over the kingship, and Cathbad's prophecy comes true.

6. *Mac Roth the Messenger*: Appropriately for a messenger, the name means 'son of wheel'.

7. *Cúailnge*: Possibly derived from *cúalne*, a stake or post. Modern Cooley in County Louth.

8. *Donn*: The designation of the Brown Bull may not be merely one of colour, but might also refer to the mythical figure known as Donn, who is associated with the dark realm of the dead.

9. *Fergus Mac Róich*: The first name means 'manly energy' and could be plausibly rendered as 'male ejaculation'. The second, unusually a matronymic, means 'son of super-horse'. Róech (Róich is the genitive) seems to have been a kind of horse-goddess. In other stories Fergus is represented as having enormous genitals and requiring seven women to satisfy him.

## II THE *TÁIN* BEGINS

1. *Cormac Conn Longas the Exile*: Literally, Cormac 'head of the exiled ones' (from *loinges*, a sea-rover or exile, derived from *long*, a ship). Frank O'Connor has suggested that there is a confusion here between Cormac and Fergus, since Cormac plays little further part in the story, and Fergus is clearly the

leader of the Ulster exiles. The story of how they were exiled is told in the *remscél* known as *Longas mac nUislenn* ('The Exile of the Sons of Uisliu', or 'Uisnech'). It may be summarized as follows:

The men of Ulster are drinking at the house of Fedlimid Mac Daill. His wife is pregnant. Everyone is about to retire to bed when the child screams out in her womb. The druid Cathbad prophesies that she will have a girl called Deirdre (Derdriu), who will be the cause of much evil. When the girl is born the Ulstermen call out for her to be killed, but their king, Conchobar, orders her to be taken away and reared in a safe place until she is ready to join him in his bed. No one is allowed to see her except her foster-parents and the satirist Leborcham (literally, 'crooked book').

One day in winter Deirdre's foster-father is skinning a calf on the snow outside, and she sees a raven drinking its blood. She says she would desire a man with those three colours: hair like the raven, cheeks like blood and his body like the snow. Leborcham lets her know that such a man is close at hand – Noisiu, the son of Uisliu. Soon afterwards she sees Noisiu alone outside the enclosure. She goes out and makes as though to pass him by and not acknowledge him. 'There's a fine heifer, to be walking past me,' he says, to which she replies, 'Heifers are wont to be big when there's no bull.' 'You have the bull of the province, the King of Ulster,' says Noisiu. 'Had I to choose between two, I'd pick a young bull like you,' says Deirdre. 'That can't be,' says Noisiu, 'on account of Cathbad's prophecy.' 'Are you refusing me?' says she. 'I am,' says he. So she grabs him by the two ears, saying, 'Two ears of shame and mockery, if you don't take me with you.' He lets a cry out of him and the men of Ulster start up ready for the kill. Uisliu's other brothers come on the scene and they all elope with Deirdre, taking a band of warriors with them.

After travelling for a long time around Ireland, pursued by Conchobar and his men, they go to Scotland, and according to one version Noisiu and Deirdre spend several happy years there. However, Conchobar lures them back to Ulster, sending Fergus Mac Róich to them as a guarantor of their safety. When Noisiu, his brothers and Deirdre arrive in Ulster Conchobar

contrives to separate Fergus from them, and sends Eogan Mac
Durthacht to attack them. Eogan kills Noisiu, and the rest are
all killed, with the exception of Deirdre. When Fergus hears of
this he goes to war with Conchobar. Among his allies are
Dubthach and Cormac. Dubthach massacres the young women
of Ulster and Fergus burns the fort of Emain. They then leave
for Connacht and the protection of Ailill and Medb.

Conchobar keeps Deirdre for a year. She is utterly miserable.
One day he asks her, 'What do you see that you hate the most?'
and she replies, 'You, and Eogan Mac Durthacht.' 'Go and live
with Eogan, then,' says Conchobar. The next day they set out
for the fair of Macha. She is behind Eogan in the chariot. 'This
is good, Deirdre,' says Conchobar. 'Between me and Eogan
you are like a sheep eyeing two rams.' A big block of stone is
in front of her. She leans out of the chariot and her head is
smashed to bits, and she dies.

2.  *the Curse*: See pp. 261–17, note 3 to Emain.

3.  *Muirthemne*: A plain extending along the coast of County
    Louth from the Boyne river to the Cooley mountains. Accord-
    ing to the *Metrical Dindshenchas*, the name means 'darkness
    of the sea' or 'under the sea's roof', since 'it was covered by
    the sea for thirty years after the Flood'.

4.  *gae bolga*: A special weapon unique to Cú Chulainn, given to
    him by the female warrior Scáthach, his tutor in the martial arts.
    It is said to have been made from the bone of a sea-monster. The
    phrase may be translated as 'the bagged spear' – suggesting
    some kind of umbrella mechanism which opens out when it
    enters its victim, and it is indeed so described in Cú Chulainn's
    combat with Fer Diad (p. 151): 'This was what the *gae bolga*
    was: it was cast downstream for him, and was thrown from
    the fork of the foot; it made a single wound when it entered a
    man's body, whereupon it opened up into thirty barbs, and it
    could not be taken from a man's body without the flesh being
    cut away from around it.' Fer Diad dies when Cú Chulainn
    penetrates 'the rear portal of his body' with the *gae bolga*. Philip
    Bernhardt-House, on his website at www.liminalityland.com,
    emphasizing the arguably homoerotic relationship between
    Cú Chulainn and Fer Diad, has this to say: '*bolga* either
    means "sack" or "swell"; thus the *gae bolga* is "the spear of

swelling" (an erect penis) or "the spear of the sack" (penis and scrotum); somewhat vulgarly put, it is quite literally "the gay bulge".' Others suggest that the name derives from the mysterious tribe known as the Fir Bolg, who in turn are associated with the continental Celtic tribe, the Belgae. Some support for this theory can be found in Diodorus Siculus' description of a somewhat similar weapon used by the Gauls: 'the heads of their javelins come from the forge straight, others twist in and out in spiral shapes for their entire length, the purpose being that the thrust may not only cut the flesh, but mangle it as well, and that the withdrawal of the spear may lacerate the wound.'

5.   *the Torqued Man*: As yet, we have not been told of Cú Chulainn's most notable attribute, the *riastradh* or 'act of twisting or contorting', famously translated by Kinsella as 'warp-spasm'; but we may be sure that it was familiar to an Old Irish audience, as it will be to many readers of the present text. My translation of *riastradh*, 'the Torque', implying both a twisting or rotating force and the Celtic ornament of twisted metal, was partly suggested by a passage in Christophe Vielle's essay, 'The Oldest Narrative Attestations of a Celtic Mythical and Traditional Heroic Cycle' (in Mallory and Stockman, *Ulidia*, Belfast, 1994). Vielle directs us to a Roman chronicle of an episode alleged to have occurred in the Gaulish war of 361 BC, in which an anonymous Gaulish warrior and the Roman general Titus Manlius meet each other in single combat. Standing in the middle of a stream, the Gaul throws out a challenge, shouting with all his strength and arousing great fear in the opposing army. When the challenge is accepted by Titus, the Gaul begins to contort himself: his appearance becomes monstrous, he dances exultantly, sticks out his tongue and hurls insults at his opponent. The Roman stands quietly, biding his time, and when the Gaul approaches him he dispatches him with one blow. Then he cuts off his head, tears off his torque, covered as it is with blood, and puts it around his own neck. He is subsequently known as Titus Manlius Torquatus, 'the Torqued One', or 'the Torqued Man'.

6.   *Deda's followers and clan*: The Clann Deda are said to have been one of the three warrior races of Ireland, the others being

the Clann Rudraige (i.e. the Ulaid or Ulstermen) and the Gamanrad.

## III THEY GET TO KNOW
## ABOUT CÚ CHULAINN

1. *Gailéoin*: A tribe based in North Leinster. In the pseudo-historical *Lebor Gabála* ('The Book of Invasions') they are mentioned as a sub-division of the Fir Bolg, and hence one of the original tribes to have invaded Ireland.

2. *Dubthach*: Also known as Doél Uladh, the Beetle of Ulster, or Doéltheangach, the Beetle-tongued. Though he is one of Fergus's exile band, his relationship with them is problematic, and he is much given to backbiting and sarcastic speech.

3. *Since two swineherds once were friends*: The reference is to one of the *remscéla* or prefatory tales to the *Táin*, *De chophur in dá muccida* ('The Quarrel of the Two Swineherds'), found in the 'Book of Leinster'. Ochall is the King of the Connacht *síd* (fairy people), Bodb the King of the Munster *síd*. Their swineherds are, respectively, Rucht (meaning 'a grunt') and Friuch ('a boar's bristle'). They both have magical powers, and can transform themselves into any shape. The two are great friends, but trouble is caused between them when people begin to argue as to which has the greater power. They quarrel and turn successively into birds of prey, water creatures, stags, warriors, phantoms and dragons, fighting each other every step of the way. Finally they turn themselves into maggots. One gets into the source of the river Cronn in Cúailnge, where it is drunk by a cow belonging to Dáire Mac Fiachna; the other gets into a well-spring in Connacht, where it is drunk by one of Ailill's and Medb's cows. The offspring of the two cows are the two bulls which feature in the *Táin*, the Donn Cúailnge and Finnbennach. So the quarrel is perpetuated.

4. *Nemain – the Battle Goddess*: Old Irish texts cite three goddesses of war: the Nemain, the Badb and the Mórrígan, sometimes known collectively as Mórrígna. They may all be aspects of the same deity.

5. *ogam*: There are many competing theories regarding this ancient form of Irish writing, reputedly invented by Ogma, the god of rhetoric and eloquence. It has been seen as a secret language of druidic freemasonry; as having its basis variously in Basque, Old Norse or Ancient Greek; or as being a musical or mathematical notation rather than a linguistic one. However, it is commonly thought to be an adaptation of the Latin alphabet, transliterated as a series of twenty combinations of straight lines and notches carved on the edge of a piece of stone or wood. Most ogam inscriptions are very short, consisting simply of a name and patronymic; many appear to be memorials to the dead, while others mark the border between territories.

6. *Eirr and Innel ... Foich and Fochlam*: The names mean, respectively, 'warrior', 'battle-gear', 'cankerworm' and 'burrower'.

7. *Partraigi*: A tribe said to have been related to the Dumnonii, who occupied the south-west of England during the Iron Age.

8. *Cennannas*: Present-day Kells in County Meath.

9. *Láeg*: The name means 'calf'.

10. *Dechtire's son*: i.e. Cú Chulainn. Dechtire is sometimes rendered Dechtine. The story of Cú Chulainn's conception and birth is told in *Compert Con Culaind* ('The Begetting of Cú Chulainn'), an eighth-century tale. It may be summarized as follows:

   One day an immense flock of birds descends on the plain of Emain, and eats everything growing on it down to the roots. The men of Ulster take to their chariots to chase the birds away, led by Conchobar and his sister Dechtire. They chase them as far as the Boyne river. As night falls it begins to snow. They find shelter in a solitary dwelling and are made welcome by the man of the house. The men of Ulster spend the night getting drunk. The man of the house then tells them that his wife is in labour in the store-room. Dechtire goes in and helps her to give birth. At the same time a mare at the door of the house gives birth to two foals. When morning comes the house and its owners have vanished. Dechtire and the Ulstermen go back to Emain with the baby and the foals.

   They rear the baby till he becomes a young boy, but then he grows sick and dies. Dechtire is overcome with grief. She comes

home from lamenting him and asks for a drink. A cup is
brought to her and as she puts her lips to it a tiny creature slips
into the drink. Later that night she dreams that she is visited
by a man who says he is Lug Mac Ethlenn (see p. 221, note 1),
that she will bear a child by him, that it was he who brought
her to the house near the Boyne, that the boy she had reared
was his, and that he is again planted in her womb. The boy
would be called Sétanta, and the two foals should be reared
with him. Dechtire grows pregnant and is mocked by the people
of Ulster because the father of the child is not known. They
suggest that Conchobar himself might have fathered it in his
drunkenness, that night in the house near the Boyne. Conchobar gives Dechtire in marriage to Sualdam Mac Róich, Fergus's
brother. She is ashamed to go to bed with him while she is
pregnant, and is so troubled that the child miscarries. She is
miraculously made virgin again, goes to bed with Sualdam,
and eventually bears him a son called Sétanta.

# IV THE BOYHOOD DEEDS OF
# CÚ CHULAINN

1.  *Celtchar Mac Uthidir*: A leading figure in other stories in the
    Ulster Cycle. He is described as tall, grey and ugly. His special
    lance, the *Lúin Cheltchair*, has such a lust for blood that if not
    used it must be dipped in a cauldron of poison, or else it will
    burst into flames.
2.  *Eogan Mac Durthacht*: King of Fernmag (present-day Farney
    in County Monaghan). He is the killer of Noisiu in *The Exile
    of the Sons of Uisliu* (see pp. 210–12, note 1).
3.  *Emain*: Or Emain Macha, nowadays identified with Navan
    Fort, an important archaeological site two miles west of the
    city of Armagh. Two women named Macha (which as an
    impersonal noun can mean either 'an enclosure for milking
    cows' or 'a plain') are associated with the founding of the
    fortress. The lesser known legend concerns Macha the queen
    of Cimbáeth, who marks out the perimeter of the fort with her
    brooch, hence the folk etymology of *emain* (usually meaning

'twins') as *eo*, pin + *muin*, neck = brooch. The better known legend concerns Macha the wife of Crunniuc mac Agnomain, a rich Ulster landlord. At a fair he boasts that his wife can run faster than the king's chariot and horses. He is taken before the king and his wife is sent for. She is pregnant and near her term, and asks to be released from the contest, but is told that unless she complies her child will die. She races the chariot and as it reaches the end of the field she gives birth to twins along-side it. Hence Emain Macha, Macha's Twins. As she gives birth she screams out that all who hear the scream will suffer the same pangs for five days and four nights in their time of greatest difficulty. The Ulstermen are so cursed for nine generations. Only young boys, women and Cú Chulainn are exempt, though why he should be singled out is not clear, beyond the fact that otherwise the *Táin* as we know it would not exist, since much of the action involves Cú Chulainn's defending the province while the Ulstermen lie smitten by the Curse.

4. *Scáthach . . . Emer*: Both women feature in the story *Tochmarc Emire* ('The Wooing of Emer'). The men of Ulster, jealous of their wives' and daughters' passion for Cú Chulainn, decide that a wife must be found for him. Messengers are sent to every part of Ireland but after searching for a year they can find no one to suit him. Cú Chulainn then meets and woos Emer, the daughter of Forgall Monach. She tells him that he cannot have her unless he manages to perform a series of seemingly impossible feats. Forgall Monach is not pleased to hear that his daughter has been wooed by Cú Chulainn. He suggests to him that if he goes to Scotland to study the martial arts under the female warrior Scáthach, he would have the beating of any hero in Europe. He does this in the hope that Cú Chulainn will never return. Cú Chulainn spends some time in Scotland. He sleeps with Scáthach's daughter Uathach and with the woman warrior Aífe, who bears him a son, and learns from Scáthach the feats detailed in the *Táin* (see p. 87). On his return to Ireland he attempts to contact Emer, but so carefully is she guarded by her father that it takes him a year to reach her. When he reaches Forgall's fort he uses his 'salmon-leap' to jump across its three enclosures. Then he fulfils his promise to perform the seemingly impossible feats required of him by

Emer, killing, among many others, her three brothers. He picks up Emer and her foster-sister and their weight in gold and silver, and leaps back over the ramparts. Eventually, after more slaughter of their pursuers, he reaches Emain and marries Emer.

5. *chess*: *Fidchell*, literally 'wood-intelligence' (i.e. as in a wood of trees). Although often translated as 'chess' we have little idea as to how the game might have worked, beyond its being played with pieces on a board.

6. *Sliab Fúait*: The Fews Mountains in South Armagh.

7. *hurley-stick*: The modern Gaelic game of hurling is a field game involving two teams of fifteen players using a broad-bladed stick ('hurley') and a ball similar to a baseball, but lighter and with a raised seam. Hurling is sometimes compared to field hockey, but as well as being played on the ground the ball may be caught or lifted into the hand and struck into the air, and play often moves from one end of the field to the other in three or four seconds. Hence it is sometimes dubbed 'the fastest field game in the world'. The goalposts are similar to those in rugby. Three points are awarded if the ball goes under the bar, and one if it goes above the bar. The All-Ireland Hurling Final, played in Croke Park, Dublin, attracts crowds of some 80,000. Hurling is also dubbed 'the oldest field game in the world', though what relationship the present-day sport might bear to that played by Cú Chulainn can only be a matter for speculation.

8. *Follomain*: 'Ruler' or 'governor'.

9. *Sétanta*: The name is possibly related to the Setantii, a Celtic tribe reported by Ptolemy as inhabiting an area in modern Lancashire; a group of them may have settled across the Irish Sea in County Louth. It is thought that they had an eponymous god, Sentonotius, meaning 'wayfarer', which fits the possible derivation of Sétanta from *sét*, a path or a way.

10. *Bricriu*: An important figure in the Ulster Cycle, and the chief protagonist of the story *Fled Bricrenn* (Bricriu's Feast). He is often given the epithet *nemthengach*, 'venom-tongued'. His name is derived from *breac*, 'speckled', cognate with English 'break'. His role as a satirist and mischief-maker is no doubt related to the designation of *breac* in some early Irish sources

as a type of satiric poetry consisting of mixed praise and vituperation.

11. *Badb*: Literally, 'scald-crow'. See p. 214, note 4.

12. *your name shall be Cú Chulainn, the Hound of Culann*: *Cú* is usually translated as 'hound'. As a generic term it may be applied to any canine, such as dog and wolf. *Culann* is a smith, and possibly one who specializes in chariot-work, since *cul* is 'chariot'.

13. *We know Cathbad well*: Cathbad is Conchobar's father (see pp. 209–10, note 5).

14. *Ibor*: 'Yew-tree'.

15. *Loch Echtra*: 'The lake of exploits'.

16. *Riddling-Rod*: *Del chliss*, 'dart of feats' or 'rod of tricks'.

# V GUERRILLA TACTICS

1. *Síd*: Cited in English as sidhe. The fairy mound is an entrance into the Otherworld, associated with features of the Irish landscape such as barrows, tumuli or man-made hillocks of ancient origin. Oral tradition has it that they mark places where the semi-divine Tuatha Dé Danann fled underground after their defeat by the mortal Milesians. 'Banshee' (*bean sídhe*) means 'fairy woman'.

2. *Maenén*: 'Dumb bird'.

3. *Morrígan, the Nightmare Queen*: 'Great queen'; alternatively 'phantom queen' or 'nightmare queen'. Like the Badb, she is associated with the crow, and sometimes manifests herself in that form. See p. 214, note 4.

4. *Forgaimen – the Skin Rug*: As an impersonal noun, glossed in *DIL* as 'a skin covering or rug used in a chariot'.

5. *Cuillius*: 'Loathsome fly', from *cuil* (a fly) + *lius* (loathsome). There are possible puns on *cul* (a chariot), and *col*, sometimes rendered *cuil* (a sin or transgression).

6. *Ailill sent for Fergus to play chess*: As shown by the exchange of *rosc* which follows, the game is metaphorical as well as literal. The dialogue accords well with Diodorus Siculus' observations on the Gauls: 'When they meet together they converse

with few words and in riddles, hinting darkly at things for the
most part and using one word when they mean another.'

7.  *draughts*: *Búanbach*, a type of board game, from *búan*, 'good'
    or 'constant', with a possible meaning of 'constant capture'.
    Like *fidchell* (see p. 218, note 5), we have little idea as to how
    it was played.

## VI SINGLE COMBAT

1.  *Etarcomol*: *Etar* (among or between) + *comol* (compact or
    agreement). A nice example of the name fitting the context:
    Etarcomol breaks his compact with Fergus not to insult Cú
    Chulainn; and Cú Chulainn is accused by Fergus of violating
    his protection of Etarcomol. For his sins Etarcomol receives an
    appropriate retribution of being cut in half.
2.  *Ed and Leithrenn*: The primary meaning of *ed* is 'it'. As a reply
    to a question, it is often translated as 'yes'. *Leithrenn* may be
    translated as 'half-share'.
3.  *Nad Crantail*: A plausible translation is 'shaft sticking out of
    arse', which is appropriate to his eventual fate at the hands of
    Cú Chulainn.

## VII THEY FIND THE BULL

1.  *Buide Mac Báin*: 'Yellow, son of white'.
2.  *Redg*: *Redg* is glossed by *DIL* as 'a sudden impulsive movement
    (inspired by anger, fear, etc.)'; the adjective *redgach* as 'easily
    startled or irritated, irascible'.
3.  *Bile Medba, Medb's Mast*: *Bile*, a tree or mast, used especially
    of an ancient and venerated tree.
4.  *the list of his feats*: Much of the list is couched in a perhaps
    deliberately obscure language to give the air of a magical incan-
    tation. Though not marked as such, it appears to be a kind of
    *rosc*. The translation is necessarily speculative. A similar list
    appears in *Tochmarc Emire* ('The Wooing of Emer').
5.  *Fer Báeth*: 'Foolish man'.
6.  *a young woman*: This section of the Irish text is titled *Imacal-*

*laim na Morrígna fri Cuin Chulaind* ('The Colloquy of the Morrígan with Cú Chulainn').

7.  *Lóch*: *Lóch* can mean variously 'bright', 'chaff' or 'reward'. Perhaps his name is a play on all three meanings.

8.  *Long*: *Long*, 'a ship'; 'a vessel or container'.

9.  *Tarteisc*: The name is ambiguous, or garbled. Kinsella renders it as 'across your water'.

10. *rear portal*: The Irish word is *timthirecht*, the verbal noun of *do-imtheret*, 'administers, serves'. DIL glosses *timthirecht* as I: 'the act of going to and fro', 'ministration'; and II: 'anus'.

## VIII THE GREAT SLAUGHTER

1.  *Lug Mac Ethlenn*: The Celtic god of light and the arts, whose name is commemorated in that of many European cities, such as Lyon, Leiden, Laon and Liegnitz (Legnica). He often bears the epithets *lámhfhada* (long-armed) and *samhildánach* (summer-skilled in all the arts). He has given his name to the Irish festival of Lughnasa (Lammas, held on 1 August, according to the Gregorian calendar). His matronymic, Mac Ethlenn, is sometimes rendered Mac Ethnenn, i.e. son of Eithne or Ethliu, daughter of Balor of the Evil Eye, whom Lug eventually kills.

2.  *Samain*: From *sam* (summer) + *fuin* (end), the most important of the four great Celtic festivals, held on 1 November. At this time, the mid-point of the Celtic year, the borders between the natural and supernatural worlds were thought to dissolve, and spirits from the Otherworld could move freely into the realm of mortals. Many of the rituals associated with Halloween are a survival of those beliefs. The other three festivals are Imbolc (see below); Beltaine, literally 'fires of Bel or Baal', held on 1 May; and Lughnasa (see above).

3.  *Imbolc*: Literally, 'swelling forth', the spring festival held on 1 February, sometimes rendered Óimelc, 'time of ewes coming into milk'. Traditionally the pagan fire-goddess Brigit has been associated with this festival, now Christianized as St Brigid's day. Brigid is the patron of sheep, of the pastoral economy and of fertility in general.

4.  *since the young maidens were slain*: A reference to Dubthach's exploits in 'The Exile of the Sons of Uisliu'. At the same time he killed Fiacha and Coirpre.
5.  *Ferchú*: *Fer* (man) + *cú* (dog or hound).
6.  *Calatín*: Possibly from *calad*, 'hard' or 'exacting'.
7.  *Glas Mac Delga*: 'Lock the son of spike'.

# IX THE COMBAT OF CÚ CHULAINN AND FER DIAD

1.  *Fer Diad*: 'One man of a couple'. Another possible interpretation is 'man of smoke'.
2.  *Fomorian giant*: The Fomorians were a mythological race with supernatural powers. Their designation in Irish, *fomoiri*, originally meant 'underworld phantoms', but because of a confusion with the archaic word *mor* with *muir* (sea) they came to be thought of as a monstrous sea-people.
3.  *The daughters of the Red Branch*: I.e. the Ulsterwomen. The Ulster Cycle was previously known as the Red Branch Cycle, from the translation of Cráebruad, one of Conchobar's three residences, so called from its large red roof-beam.
4.  *Banba*: A personification of Ireland, one of three such divine eponyms, the others being Éiriu and Fódla.

# XIII THE FINAL BATTLE

1.  *stark naked*: As Diodorus Siculus remarks of the Gauls, 'certain of them despise death to such a degree that they enter the perils of battle with no more than a girdle about their loins'.
2.  *Én*: 'Bird'.
3.  *Léte's sword*: Léte was the father of Fergus.
4.  *The pot was stirred, Fergus, and today a mess was made*: *Correcad lochta agus fulachta sund inniu, a Fhergais*. My translation is based on Ann Dooley's reading in 'The Invention of Women in the Táin' (in Mallory & Stockman, *Ulidia*, Belfast, 1994):

O'Rahilly has provided only a very tentative translation of this phrase, 'Men and lesser men meet here today, Fergus', taking *locht* as meaning 'group of individuals'; she indicated that she felt it was some kind of proverbial phrase, the import of which is not clear. One might also read *locht* as 'defect', hence the notion of the expedition as well and truly messed up. A better, or at least alternative reading might begin with *fulachta*, 'cooking-pits' and note the common usage of *locht* as the contents of the cooking vessel, thus yielding a variation on 'the fat is in the fire' idea. This has the advantage of bringing us closer to two terms through which one might access the scene of Medb's urination. *DIL* lists, besides *fulachtad*, 'cooking', *fulachtad*, 'bloodletting'; in addition, one has the common phrase, *fulacht fian/fiadh* to describe various obvious pits or small-scale features of landscape as well as the literary term *fulacht na Morrigna*.